This book provided
through the

ÀSONGOÛT

TRUST

Death Rides A Black Horse

Death Rides
A Black Horse

LEWIS B. PATTEN

DOUBLEDAY & COMPANY, INC.
GARDEN CITY, NEW YORK
1978

003 635 284

All of the characters in this book are fictitious, and any
resemblance to actual persons, living or dead, is purely
coincidental.

ISBN: 0-385-14008-8
Library of Congress Catalog Card Number 77-16851

Chapter I

My father's name was Walter Halliday. He was a giant of a man who had carved the Halliday Ranch out of Wyoming grassland when no one else wanted it or, indeed, even dared cross it without an escort of cavalry. That was in sixty-five, the year after the Sand Creek Massacre. For several years afterward the Cheyennes rampaged across the high plains, killing, raiding, exacting revenge for the unprovoked slaughter. Twice, my father and mother and Rafe Joslin forted up inside the sod shack that was their first dwelling and fought off raiding parties.

In sixty-seven, Custer attacked a village of Cheyennes down south on the Washita and wiped it out. After that, maybe the tribe accepted the inevitable because the raiding mostly stopped. Then, in seventy-six, the Sioux killed most of Custer's command at the Little Big Horn. That defeat probably did more to pacify the plains than a victory could have done.

I was born in sixty-four, the year of the Sand Creek Massacre. I was a year old when Father and Mother built the sod shack and settled what would grow into the Halliday Ranch. Rafe Joslin drifted by a year later, stopped for the night and stayed.

In seventy-nine, the year of my father's death, I was

fifteen. It was July and the school in the town of Halliday
had closed for the summer. My mother had been dead for
nearly ten years and the house was run by a Mexican
woman named Dolores Rivera. She was middle-aged and
heavy. Her dark skin showed that she had plenty of Indian
blood. She was smiling and cheerful. She kept the house
clean and cooked for Pa and me and for Rafe, our foreman
now, who lived in the house with us instead of out in the
bunkhouse with the crew.

Father was six feet two and at the time of his death
weighed two hundred and twenty pounds. I might eventually be as big, but at fifteen, because I was beginning to
shoot up, I was skinny as a rail and didn't weigh much
more than a hundred pounds.

The day of Father's death was like any other summer day
except that along toward dusk his horse came in, dusty, a
leg broken, the saddle badly scratched, plainly from a fall.
Rafe Joslin told one of the crew to unsaddle the horse, take
him out to a gully a mile from the house and put him out of
his misery. He organized a crew of six men to backtrack the
horse. By then it was dark and necessary to use a lantern to
read trail. I was included, of course, and we left as soon as
we got organized, less than twenty minutes after Pa's horse
came in.

I believed that he was hurt. It never occurred to me that
he might be dead. To me he was like one of the great stone
buttes that dotted our H Quarter Circle range, unchangea-
ble and indestructible.

Rafe Joslin led out, with me right behind. The others, six
in all, followed. Beside Rafe, who carried the lantern, rode
Jack Standing Bear, who broke horses for the ranch. He
was the best tracker on the place.

Except for the difficulty of seeing the ground by lantern
light, the trail wasn't hard to follow owing to the fact that

Father's horse had been carrying a broken leg, hopping along on the other three. But the going was slow. I had plenty of time to think.

My relationship with my father was not what you would have called a warm one. He was a hard, outwardly cold man, who had built what he had with a combination of backbreaking work and uncompromising toughness. He expected as much from his hired hands and from me as he did from himself.

I was only five when my mother died, so I wasn't even aware of him taking up with Rose Moran. I learned later that, two years after Mother died, he fixed up an abandoned homesteader's house about three miles from the ranch and moved her into it. Why he didn't just bring her home, or marry her, I never understood. He didn't give a damn what people thought, but maybe he believed that marrying again would somehow be unfaithful to my mother's memory.

Anyway, he supported Rose, and visited her a couple of times a week. I was old enough to understand his physical need for her, but I knew he had a real affection for her too. Otherwise, she would not have stayed. The truth was, she loved him deeply and, while she would have preferred being married to him, she was willing to take whatever she could of him just so she didn't have to give him up. I had only met her once, by accident, and I'd liked her immediately.

At fifteen, I did a man's work. I went to school in the wintertime, but in the morning I had my chores and I had chores when I came home from school at night. Summers, I worked from dawn to dark just like everybody else.

Despite my father's apparent coldness, I knew he felt some affection toward me and I thought he approved of me. I know I tried hard to measure up to what he expected from me. I wanted his approval and worked hard at earning it.

At a slow walk, because of the necessity of reading trail,

we rode for almost ten miles. The hours dragged, but at last Rafe Joslin stopped, dismounted and knelt. I slid off my horse and ran forward. By the lantern's light I saw that Rafe and Jack Standing Bear were kneeling beside my father, lying twisted and motionless on the ground.

Rafe put his hand on Father's chest. He looked up, glanced first at Standing Bear and then at me. He shook his head.

It was several moments before I could comprehend that my father, such an indestructible giant, was really dead. And from a stupid accident like having a horse fall with him. Even when I understood, I could not accept the reality of it. I kept thinking it was a bad dream from which I would soon awake.

It took four men to lift him and lay him across the saddle of a horse. All the men were shocked, talking only in whispers among themselves. Rafe and Jack Standing Bear lashed my father's body down. We started back toward the ranch house, traveling at a walk.

Numb and stunned, I rode with the men. I found myself wishing that, just once, my father had told me he approved of me. Maybe his failure to do so was as much my fault as his, though, because I had always been in such awe of him that I'd found it impossible to talk to him. I'd never confided in him or taken any of my troubles to him.

And now it was too late. We reached the ranch at midnight. The men carried Father in and laid him on the long, leather-covered sofa in the living room. Dolores lighted a lamp and brought it in. The men backed out respectfully, their faces solemn. Rafe sent one of them to town to bring the undertaker's hearse.

Rafe and Dolores dressed Father in his black Sunday suit. Then Rafe and I sat with him for the rest of the night. I kept glancing at my father's face from time to time, as if by some miracle he would come to life. Finally, as dawn began to streak the sky, the hearse arrived and six of the crewmen carried Father's body out to it and laid it carefully inside. The hearse, drawn by four black horses, drove away.

Standing there in the cool of dawn, Rafe turned and looked at me. He seemed as numb and unbelieving as I felt. He said hoarsely, "Go on to bed, Frank. Get some sleep. This afternoon we'll ride into town and make the arrangements for his funeral."

Rafe was a wiry, tough, hard-muscled man, five feet ten inches tall. His eyes were close-set, his mouth a thin, straight line. In my mind he was as much a part of the Halliday Ranch as my father had been. That was not surprising, since he'd been its foreman for fourteen years.

I went in and went to bed. Dolores awakened me at noon. She had dinner on by the time I got myself dressed and washed and got to the table.

Rafe and I ate alone. The crew was eating in the bunkhouse. By the time we had finished, they were ready, waiting in the yard, dressed in their Sunday best. A buckboard had been readied, a black team hitched to it. Rafe drove and I sat beside him all the way to town.

We drove to the undertaker's parlor, which was in a store building that adjoined the hardware store and was owned by the man who owned the hardware store. Pa was lying in a casket lined with white satin, his hands folded on his chest. His face was very pale, his eyes closed. Looking at him, I felt my throat close up and felt tears come to my eyes.

Rafe and Mr. Hawkins, the undertaker, talked, agreeing on two o'clock the following day for the funeral. Rafe and I drove back home with the whole crew following along behind in a column of twos.

When we got home I asked Rafe about Rose Moran. I

said she didn't even know that Pa was dead, much less about the arrangements for the funeral.

His face turned hard when I mentioned her name. He said, "To hell with her!" in a tone I didn't want to argue with.

But I figured Pa would have wanted Rose to know. He would have wanted her at his funeral. It was cruel to leave her in ignorance of his death, no matter whether you approved of their relationship or not. The fact of the matter was, I didn't figure it was up to me either to approve or disapprove. No matter how Rafe looked at it.

So I saddled a horse and rode out as soon as Rafe had disappeared into the house. I headed directly for Rose's place.

It was a small, two-room cabin, built of pine logs that the original builder must have freighted from the mountains more than twenty miles away. It was well cared for, and that, I supposed, was Father's doing. He had probably sent a crewman over whenever something needed to be fixed.

But the small lawn and the flowers and climbing vines were things that Rose had done herself. The sun was about to set when I rode up to her house and dismounted in front of it. There was a hitching post and I tied my horse to it.

Rose came out of the door as I opened the picket gate and went up the path toward it. She must have been able to tell from my face that something was wrong. Or else the fact that I was there was enough to tell her something was wrong.

The color went out of her face and her eyes looked scared. I knew I ought to tell her tactfully but I didn't know how, so I just blurted, "Miss Moran, my father's dead."

She grasped one of the porch pillars to steady herself. For an instant she stared at me and then her eyes filled with tears that spilled over and ran down across her cheeks.

She seemed to have forgotten I was there. An expression of intense pain crossed her face. I said, "Miss Moran!" and hurried to her and took hold of her arm.

Her arm was soft and she smelled good. I helped her into the house, on through the kitchen and into the bedroom beyond. She let me help her to the bed and she sat down on the edge of it.

She looked up and tried to smile, but it was a wan and pitiful effort. "Thank you, Frank. I'm sorry. It came as such a shock."

I didn't say anything, because I didn't know what to say. She asked, "How? And when?"

"Yesterday. His horse came in just before dark last night. We spent the whole night finding him and bringing his body home. We went to bed and slept till noon and then Rafe an' I went in and made the funeral arrangements with Mr. Hawkins in town."

"When is the funeral to be?"

"Two o'clock tomorrow."

She nodded. I thought she probably wanted to be alone so that she could weep, so I said, "Well, I got to be going."

She got up. "I'll see you to the door."

I went back through the kitchen to the door. She followed and when I reached it, said, "Thank you for coming, Frank."

"You're welcome, ma'am." I went to my horse, untied him and mounted. I looked back but she had disappeared and the door was closed. I turned to ride away, hearing as I did her awful, tearing sobs of grief.

I felt tears coming to my own eyes from hearing her. It didn't take long to get back home. I hoped Rafe wouldn't ask me about where I'd been, and he didn't.

The next morning nobody did any work. At noon the crew was ready, dressed in the best clothes they had. One of the men brought the buckboard to the back door. Rafe mounted to the seat and took up the reins. Dolores Rivera got up beside him and I squeezed in beside her. She cried off and on all the way to town, sometimes dabbing at her eyes with a handkerchief.

It was the first funeral I'd ever attended. It was held in the Methodist Church at the upper end of town. The preacher, David Thorne, talked about what a fine man my father had been, God-fearing and hard-working. He spoke of him as a pioneer, without whom the town of Halliday would not exist.

The casket was open and when the funeral was over, everybody walked past it and looked at him, paying their last respects. I turned my head as I went by and saw Rose Moran waiting at the back of the church so that she could be the last one to walk past the casket. Her face was covered by a black veil and she was dressed all in black but she was unmistakable.

I was one of the pallbearers. We all waited in the small vestibule until the mourners had left. Rose was the last one out. She glanced at me, then ducked her head and hurried past.

I was thinking that not all these people had liked my father and a lot of them had resented the amount of land he held, some of it only by right of possession. But they all had respected him and their faces showed it now. I thought that filling his shoes was going to be a mighty big job. I wasn't sure I could.

The pallbearers, of whom Rafe was also one, carried the casket out to the hearse. Then we walked behind it up the hill to the cemetery, some of the mourners walking behind, some dispersing and going home. Rose Moran was one of those who came.

The preacher said a few words at the graveside, and then

the casket was lowered in and a shovelful of earth thrown
on top of it.

In the silence that followed, I could hear Rose weeping.
Rafe stared across the open grave at her, his face hard and
without sympathy.

I wanted to volunteer to drive Rose home but Rafe said,
"Julius Larrabee wants to see us in his office, Frank. He
wants to read your father's will."

I hadn't thought about the will or about what was going
to happen to the Halliday Ranch now that he was dead.
Rafe stared coldly at Rose, then said reluctantly to me, "He
wants to see that woman too. Do you mind telling her?"

I didn't mind. I walked to where Rose was standing,
turning my hat nervously around and around in my hands. I
said, "Miss Moran, Julius Larrabee wants to see you and
me and Rafe Joslin in his office. He's going to read my father's will."

"I don't want . . ." She stopped.

I said, "Please, ma'am. When it's over, I'll drive you
home."

She nodded. "All right." I walked beside her down the
hill and back into the town. We were the last two. Rafe and
the crew and all the other mourners were ahead of us.

Thinking about the will, I supposed that part of the ranch
would now belong to me. Part would undoubtedly be left to
Rafe, since he was almost as much a part of it as my father
had been.

At the bottom of the hill, Rafe told the crewmen they
could have the rest of the day off. They immediately headed
for the saloon, stopping at the church as they went by to
untie and mount their horses they'd left tied there earlier.

Rafe got up into the buckboard and looked expectantly
at me, waiting for me to help Dolores and climb up beside

her for the drive downtown. I shook my head. "I'll drive Miss Moran."

Rafe scowled, but he reached a hand down for Dolores and pulled her up to the seat. I untied Miss Moran's buggy horse. She was already in the buggy, so I didn't have to help her. I got in and drove after Rafe and Dolores.

I slapped the horse's back lightly with the reins and he broke into a trot, keeping pace with Rafe's team. Rose Moran said, "Thank you for coming with me. It's awkward." She hesitated a moment and then said, "You knew your father and I were friends?"

"Yes, ma'am."

"For a very long time. Nearly eight years, in fact."

"Yes ma'am. I knew."

"He probably never told you, Frank, but he was very proud of you."

I said, "He never told me."

"He wasn't one to speak his feelings. But he had them, Frank. Very deep ones, whether he spoke them or not."

I was glad to hear how he'd felt about me. I said, "Thanks for telling me, Miss Moran."

"It's *Mrs*. Moran, Frank. I'm a widow."

"Yes, ma'am." In silence then, we drove the last couple of blocks to Julius Larrabee's office in the center of town.

Chapter II

Julius Larrabee's office was in a two-story brick building. It was reached by an outside stairway leading to the second floor. Rafe left Dolores sitting in the buckboard and climbed the stairs by himself. I helped Rose Moran out of the buggy and followed her up the stairs. Rafe didn't bother to hide the fact that he neither liked nor approved of her.

Larrabee's office was the first one on the left. The second belonged to Doc Hoffman. The two offices on the right, facing the alley, were vacant.

Larrabee's desk was littered with papers. He was a short, paunchy man, who always wore a black serge suit with shiny elbows and a shiny place on the seat of the pants. He had a black vest, across which was a heavy gold chain. On one end of it, tucked into his vest pocket, was a gold watch with an engraved gold hunting case, and in the opposite pocket was a small gold penknife that he used to cut off the ends of his cigars.

He stood up when Rose came in and told us all to sit down. He rummaged in his safe for several moments, then brought some papers out. He began to read, after explaining that it was my father's will. Rose's face was drawn and pale. Rafe's was, as usual, expressionless. Mr. Larrabee read, "I, Walter Halliday, being of sound mind, do hereby . . ." It went on for a long time before it got down to anything specific. He left amounts from a hundred to a thousand dollars to various crew members who had worked at the ranch a long time. He left Rafe five thousand dollars. He left Rose Moran the house she lived in and the forty acres upon which it sat, along with a monthly income of fifty dollars for the rest of her life.

I glanced at Rafe's face. It was like carved granite. Five thousand dollars sounded like a lot of money to me and I thought he should have been pleased. Apparently he was not.

Rose had tears in her eyes and I had the feeling she was not only pleased, but touched that Father had remembered and provided for her.

Larrabee's droning voice continued. He came at last to the ranch and cattle and the remaining cash in the Halliday bank. That was all placed in trust for me until I would be twenty-one. My father appointed Rafe trustee. When I became twenty-one, all of it would pass to me. In the meantime, Rafe was requested to stay on as foreman and continue running the ranch as he had in the past. In addition to his regular salary, he was to get a hundred dollars a month for acting as trustee.

Sitting there listening, I thought that my life wasn't going to change much. I'd keep on going to school, doing chores morning and night while I did, and working full time in the summer. Rafe's life wouldn't change much either except that he'd get paid more and except that he'd have five thousand dollars that he hadn't had before.

Larrabee hadn't quite finished reading the will. He had stopped but he wasn't looking either at it or at me. He was looking at Rafe. I glanced at Rafe and saw that his face was red. His eyes were narrowed and his mouth was an even thinner line than usual. Rafe was furious. I had seen him angry before and I knew the signs.

Larrabee said, "I'm sorry, Rafe. I tried . . ."

Rafe's voice came out tight and strange. "I gave him my life! I worked my ass off for him the last fifteen years. Hell, I did as much to build the Halliday Ranch as he did, and this is what I get for it!"

Larrabee said, "There's one more paragraph."

Rafe was silent. I was embarrassed and uncomfortable. Rose looked as if she'd rather be anyplace but here. Larrabee read, "In the event of Rafael Joslin's death before my son reaches twenty-one, Rose Moran is requested to take over his duties as trustee."

I was afraid to even look at Rafe, but I couldn't help myself. His face looked as if he was about to explode. Larrabee's droning voice went on, "In the event of my son's death before he comes of age, title to all the above-mentioned property shall pass to my faithful foreman and friend, Rafael Joslin. Lastly, it is my wish that my son, Frank Halliday, retain Rafael Joslin as foreman of Halliday Ranch for the remainder of his life."

Larrabee's voice stopped. He laid the will down upon his desk. "That's all."

Rose Moran stood up. So did Rafe and I. I shook Mr. Larrabee's hand and so did Rose. Rafe just stared at him. Without waiting for Rose, Rafe went out, slamming the door thunderously behind.

Mr. Larrabee said, "He should have had more. He should have had part of the ranch."

I said, "I'll give it to him."

"You can't. You won't have title to anything until you're twenty-one."

Rose went out onto the landing and I followed her. Rafe was driving down the street with the buckboard horses at a gallop, with Dolores clinging to the seat with both her hands.

I turned and looked back at Mr. Larrabee, who had followed us out. I asked, "Couldn't I tell him that I'm going to give him part of it as soon as I can?"

"You could, but it wouldn't mean anything. It wouldn't be binding and you could change your mind any time you wanted to in the next six years."

Rose touched my arm. "He'll get over it."

I supposed she was right. I followed her down the stairs and helped her into her buggy. I untied the horse and climbed in beside her. Being so close to her was pleasant and I could understand why she had meant so much to my father and why he had seen her so regularly. I drove down the street and out of town, very conscious of the curious stares Rose got from everyone we passed.

Neither of us spoke for a long time. Finally Rose asked, "I embarrass you, don't I, Frank?"

I shook my head. "No, ma'am. It's just that I'm not used to being around women, especially when they're as pretty as you. I'm used to Dolores and to Miss Pritchett, the teacher. You're different."

"You mean because your father and I were . . ."

"No, ma'am." I turned my head and looked at her. "Rafe doesn't like you or approve of you. But that's no reason you and me can't be friends."

She smiled. She said, "I'd like that, Frank, and I'm sure your father would have liked it too."

I drove her the rest of the way home. I let her out and borrowed her buggy long enough to go home and get a horse. I didn't go to the house, but to the corral. I knew Rafe was home because I saw the buckboard sitting beside the barn. The buckboard horses were in the corral, eating hay.

I caught myself a horse, tied it behind the buggy and drove back to Rose's place. I unhitched the buggy horse, watered him and put him in the stable behind the house.

She came to the door and asked me in, but I shook my head. I mounted and rode back home. I wanted to tell Rafe I was going to give him a share of the ranch, but no matter how I tried to phrase it in my mind, it always sounded condescending, like I was making a present to him. I realized that anything I said would only make him madder than he already was.

I didn't know why my father hadn't recognized it, but Rafe *had* earned a share of the Halliday Ranch. The reason I couldn't come up with a way of saying it right was that there wasn't any way. It would be insulting for me to have to give him what he had already earned.

I reached home and put my horse away. I can't explain why, but part of that last paragraph in my father's will kept running through my mind, over and over again. "In the event of my son's death before he comes of age, title to all the above-mentioned property shall pass to my faithful foreman and friend, Rafael Joslin."

As I walked toward the house, Rafe came out, carrying an armload of his things. I understood that he was moving out of the house and into the bunkhouse with the crew.

His face was cold and angry and once, when his eyes met mine, I saw pure hatred toward me in them.

For the first time, I felt a stirring of anger within myself. I had not, after all, written my father's will. I'd had nothing to do with it and hadn't even known what it said.

Furthermore, the entire ranch had belonged to my father and Rafe had only worked for him. He had been generous giving Rafe five thousand dollars in cash, his job for life, and an extra hundred a month until I turned twenty-one.

I'd still have been willing to give him part of the ranch.

But I couldn't do it legally, and doing it any other way wouldn't mean anything.

I'd just have to wait. Rafe would get over his anger, and he didn't really hate me even if he had looked at me as if he did.

I went into the house. Dolores was working in the kitchen, preparing supper. There was fright in her eyes.

I said, "Don't worry, Dolores, he'll get over it. It will just take time."

She nodded her head, but I could tell she didn't believe that what I said was true. I shouldn't have believed it either. Rafe Joslin was not the kind of man who easily forgets.

Dolores put supper on the table and we both sat down to eat. I couldn't help thinking that things were going to be pretty unpleasant for a while. Rafe was still foreman. In his present state of mind he was going to make things just as hard for me as he could.

But I could take it, or I thought I could. All I had to do was my work the same as I always had. Rafe would run the ranch itself.

I heard hoofbeats in the yard and went to the back door. It was dark, but there was a moon. A horseman was thundering out of the yard, heading up the lane, probably going to town. I knew immediately that it was Rafe. I knew the black horse he always rode, the one with the white stockings on his front feet and the white blaze on his face.

Dolores said, "He is very angry, Señor Frank."

I felt depressed, not only because of the way Rafe was acting, but because we had buried my father today. I said goodnight to Dolores and climbed the stairs to my room.

I lighted a lamp and sat down in the easy chair beside my bed. I stared at the wall, a sudden, disquieting thought running through my mind.

I was all that stood between Rafe and ownership of the

entire ranch. The will had said that if I died before I reached twenty-one, then the whole thing would go to Rafe. And Rafe was furious, angry enough to . . . I made my thoughts stop there. Rafe had known me most of my life. He might be angry and he might be disappointed that he hadn't been left a share in the ranch. But that didn't mean he'd try to kill me for it.

I suddenly realized how tired I was. I took off my clothes and got into bed. I blew out the lamp.

It was a long time before I went to sleep. And even when I did, I had nightmares that I was running from something. But I never saw what it was I was running from.

I awoke once in the early-morning hours hearing the pound of a horse's hoofs on the bare earth of the yard. I looked out the window and saw that it was Rafe. He unsaddled and put his horse away, then walked unsteadily to the bunkhouse. He disappeared inside.

I went back to bed and I didn't awaken again until dawn.

That day the crew began putting the haying machinery in order, greasing mowing machines and sharpening sickles first, afterward putting the dump rakes and buck rakes into shape and making sure the stackers worked. The following day four of the crew began to mow, starting at the outside edge of the east hayfield and working in toward the center, one following another so that, with each round, they cut a twenty-foot-wide swath.

At noon, I took over driving one of the mowers and I worked at it steadily until it was too dark to see.

I liked driving a mowing machine. I liked the smell of new-cut hay and the sweaty smell of the team. I suppose I liked the monotony of it too, making round after round, watching the hay fall behind the sickle bar.

The whole field was down. I put away my team, after watering them, and gave them both hay and oats. I went to the house feeling like an outcast because I had to eat alone.

The following morning, while the hay cured in the hot morning sun, we started cutting on the west side of the house. By noon the dump rakes were beginning on the hay cut yesterday, raking and dumping, raking and dumping, until the whole field was in neat windrows that could be picked up by buck rakes and taken to where the stacker was.

We used a slide stacker made of lodgepole pine poles from which all the bark had been removed. Pushed onto pole teeth like those on the buck rake, the hay was pulled up by a stacker team, usually driven by a boy, and at the top of the slide, dumped down upon the stack where one, two, or three men spread it out so that all four sides of the stack were straight and the corners fairly square.

It was the next day, though, before we started stacking hay. Up until this year, it had been my job to drive the stacker team. This year, Rafe put me on the stack, and let a kid from town that Dolores knew drive the stacker team.

Working on the stack is a dusty, hot, unpleasant job. Half buried by hay, into which you sink above the waist, you get little benefit from the breeze. Your nose is clogged with dust. And if there are enough buck rakes working, you're buried most of the time and have to work at top speed, without pausing, for the entire day.

Usually the men take turns, half a day on the stack, half a day driving a buck rake team. But when noon came, Rafe didn't offer to relieve me on the stack, or Lucas Richards, working at the other end. In midafternoon Rafe sent Lucas to the house for cold drinking water, leaving me on the stack alone.

I was beginning to get a foretaste of what life was going to be like for me during the next six years. Rafe was going to give me the hardest, dirtiest jobs on the ranch. Maybe he thought he'd break me and I'd run away. Or maybe it gave him some kind of satisfaction he couldn't get any other way.

Anyway, I was working at top speed, trying to keep up with the loads of hay dumped onto the stack and steadily falling behind because it just wasn't possible for one man. Rafe was driving a buck rake, and as he brought in an extra-large load and pushed it onto the stacker teeth, I caught him watching me, a peculiar expression on his face.

But I didn't have time, either to continue looking at him or to wonder what was behind his expression. I was too busy spreading hay. Rafe's load came up, dropping onto the last load that I hadn't even had time to begin to spread.

It made a pile that came almost to the top of my head, considering the way I was sinking down into the hay. And suddenly I heard a sound that turned me cold. It was unmistakable to me because I had heard it so many times before. It was the buzz of a rattler, a big one from the sound of it, and it wasn't two feet from my head.

I had my fork out in front of me preparatory to attacking that double load of piled-up hay. I jammed it into the hay and pushed myself away, falling spreadeagled on my back.

The snake struck, hampered by the fact that he was tangled up in the loose hay and not able to coil properly. He was a big one, as thick as my arm and maybe six feet long.

Only his rattle and my own swift reaction to the sound had saved me. He struck thin air, where my head had been only an instant before. I scrambled back until I could get to my feet out of the snake's striking range. I glanced down at Rafe, driving away with his buck rake and team. He was looking back at me.

The snake was now trying to get away from me, trying to lose himself in the loose hay. I jabbed at him, still feeling cold as ice, and on the third jab managed to put one of the fork tines through the thick part of his body.

I threw the fork like a javelin, snake and all, at the ground in front of the stack. The fork stuck, leaving the impaled snake writhing there. I yelled at the next man who drove the buck rake in, "Kill that damned snake and throw me back my fork."

The man got off his buck rake and killed the snake. He tossed my fork back up to me.

I went back to work, furiously trying to put one persistent memory out of my mind. The memory was of Mr. Larrabee's voice, reading my father's will. "In the event of my son's death before he comes of age . . ."

Maybe the snake coming in with Rafe's load had been an accident. Maybe Rafe's sending Lucas to the house for drinking water had been a coincidence. Furthermore, a rattlesnake bite is seldom fatal, unless, of course, it is in the face or neck.

I told myself that every haying season at least a couple of snakes came up onto the stacks in loads of hay. I told myself this was just one of those times. But I was not entirely convinced. There were too many coincidences, the first being that Rafe's load contained the snake at a time when Lucas was at the house after drinking water. The second, and more serious, was the fact that I had been a couple of loads behind, which would put Rafe's load, containing the snake, at about the level of my head.

When we quit for the night, I cut off the rattlers and put them in my shirt pocket. I didn't look at Rafe. The men were talking about the snake and the close call I'd had, while I alternated between being scared and telling myself that I was imagining things.

Chapter III

The next day, Rafe Joslin stopped me on my way out to the hayfield. There wasn't a trace of smile on his face and no friendliness in his eyes. "Guess you don't want to work on the stack after what happened yesterday."

I didn't. I knew that all day long I'd be watching every load that came up and half afraid of every step I took. I'd be listening for the rattling of a snake. But I sure as hell wasn't going to let Rafe know he'd got my goat. I shrugged. "Makes no difference to me where I work. But one man can't spread the hay from three or four buck rakes."

His expression didn't change. "All right, then. You work on the stack again. I'll put Lucas up there with you."

I rode up onto the half-built stack with the first load of hay. For a while I was as nervous as I'd expected to be, but after a while I forgot about snakes and concentrated on spreading hay and tramping it down. No snakes came up on the stack that day, or the next, or again all through haying. I worked on the stack three days in all. The rest of the time I drove a buck rake.

The summer days passed uneventfully, but as much as I tried to put that snake incident out of my mind, it stayed there, and I often caught myself wondering what Rafe was going to try next. Sometimes in the evening I'd ride out to

Rose Moran's place and we'd sit on the porch in the shade and talk. We got to be real good friends.

Every morning those of the crew that were present at the home place would gather in front of the bunkhouse and Rafe would assign them jobs for the day. It was at one of these sessions in late August that he looked at me and said, "I want you to ride over to Alkali Springs today and make sure it ain't gone dry. It usually dries up this time of year and if it has, bring back what cattle you can find. If you don't think you got 'em all, I'll send several men out that way tomorrow."

I nodded and went to the corral for my horse. The ride out to Alkali Springs would take nearly half a day. If I brought back any cattle, I wouldn't get home until well after dark. But I didn't mind. Sometimes I liked being alone, and the ride out to Alkali Springs was by no means an unpleasant one.

The strain around the ranch hadn't lessened much since my father's death. Rafe still lived in the bunkhouse with the crew. I lived in the house with Dolores, and I have to admit it got pretty lonesome. But if I went to the bunkhouse to talk to the crew, Rafe was always there, with his cold, unsmiling face, and nobody seemed anxious to talk to me. Finally I just stopped going.

During the summer, I had made up my mind to a couple of things. I had no choice but to remain and work under Rafe Joslin's orders until I was twenty-one. But when I *was* twenty-one, a lot of things were going to change. Rafe Joslin was going to go, if I had to pay him a pension for the rest of his life. I was tired of his cold hatred toward me that he no longer even tried to hide. I was angry because I didn't deserve it from him.

It was a pleasant day. The sky was blue, and there were

only a few puffy clouds above the western horizon. They'd probably build into thunderheads during the day.

The wind was blowing, of course. In our part of Wyoming the wind nearly always blew. It rippled the grass, sometimes making it look like waves. I rode at a steady trot.

I had never carried a gun while my father was alive. I was still too self-conscious about it to carry a handgun, because none of the cowhands on the ranch carried them. But I had begun carrying a Spencer carbine that had belonged to Father, thrust into a saddle scabbard under my leg. I'd been joshed a little about carrying it. But I still had the memory of that rattlesnake in my mind and I couldn't help wondering what was likely to happen next. The long summer, with nothing happening, had lulled me into a feeling that nothing more was likely to happen, that the rattlesnake episode had, indeed, been an accident. But I still took the carbine with me whenever I rode out away from the house.

A little before noon, I brought the butte that marked the location of Alkali Springs into sight. At about the same time, I crossed the trail of a number of cattle—probably, I thought, heading for the springs.

I suppose turning into the trail was automatic. I followed it for nearly half a mile before I noticed that the tracks of two horses overlaid the cattle's tracks. And then I began to notice other things. The cattle weren't traveling as if they were on their way to water, in which case they would have followed any of a number of well-worn trails made previously through the prairie grass. They were traveling in a bunch, being driven by two men on horseback. Rustlers.

As soon as I realized it, I dismounted and carefully studied the tracks. I wasn't an expert tracker, but I'd ridden with Jack Standing Bear enough so that I'd learned a little about tracking and telling how long ago a trail had been made.

In this case, the edges of the tracks were sharp, not yet blurred by wind. The droppings were shiny and fresh, and when I put my hand near to one pile of them, I could feel the warmth.

I had stumbled onto something. Now I didn't know what I ought to do. It was the first time, really, that I'd been called upon to make a decision like a man.

The smart thing, of course, would be to turn around, ride back to the ranch as fast as possible, and get reinforcements before tackling these rustlers. But it would be morning before I could get back. In the meantime, the rustlers could drive the cattle fifteen or twenty miles. They could get lost in another bunch of cattle. Their tracks could get lost in other cattle tracks.

Besides that, like my father, I hated thieves. I decided I'd follow this trail for a little while and try to get a glimpse of the rustlers. I might recognize them and they had no way of knowing I was here.

Following them was foolish of course. Thieves caught in the act of stealing almost always react violently. I was only one against two. But I suppose there was enough of my father in me to make me act as he would have acted in similar circumstances. I couldn't imagine my father going for help in a situation like this.

I rode along the trail, staring cautiously ahead, trying to get a glimpse of the cattle and the men driving them.

The country was rolling, cut by deep washes made by torrential rains pouring down the sides of the butte. I followed for ten or fifteen minutes, but saw nothing ahead.

A feeling of uneasiness began to come over me. The rustlers and their cattle should have gone over a rise or high ground and become visible by now. Unless they had seen me. Unless they were lying in wait for me.

That thought put a cold chill in my spine. Maybe it was

the thought or the chill that made me leave the saddle hastily, grabbing the Spencer out of the saddle boot as I did.

Even before my foot touched the ground, I knew I had dismounted in the nick of time. Ahead, where the land dipped slightly, I saw a puff of smoke. Almost simultaneously I heard the crack of a rifle.

They had seen me and had been waiting for me. I dropped to the ground, looking around for something to hide behind. My horse, startled by the report, trotted away, dragging the reins. He stopped after going fifty feet or so.

There was a rock half a dozen feet to my left, beside which a clump of sagebrush grew. I scrambled, crabwise, to reach it before the rustlers could shoot again.

Apparently they couldn't see me well enough from their hiding place to shoot. I saw them suddenly appear where the earlier shot had come from. Both had rifles. They were ordinary-looking men except that one had a beard.

I had reached the rock and the sagebrush clump. I knew I'd never get another chance like this. Shoving my rifle muzzle through the sagebrush clump, I lined my sights on the one with the beard and fired.

The man went back as if he had been kicked by a mule. I shifted my rifle muzzle slightly to shoot at the other one.

He was gone. He had dived out of sight when he saw his companion go down.

All of a sudden I was shaking like an aspen leaf in a high wind. I broke out in a cold sweat. At that moment I couldn't have hit the broad side of a barn. I had shot and probably killed a man.

I lay there without moving. I knew the second man could, even now, be circling, so that he could get a clear shot at me from the side or rear. I was lying on a kind of knoll. On my right there was a shallow gully, not deep enough to conceal a man if he was walking erect, but deep enough to conceal one crawling along the ground.

From ahead, there was no sound at all. I was still bathed with sweat and my hands, holding the rifle so tightly the knuckles were white, were clammy. But my trembling had lessened.

I couldn't stay where I was. If I did, sooner or later the unwounded rustler would get around in back of me.

Once I'd made up my mind, I didn't hesitate long enough to give myself time to doubt. I got up and, half running, half crawling, plunged away from the cover of the rock and sagebrush clump toward the shallow gully on my right. Maybe I'd run smack into the other rustler. But the gully offered the only reliable cover I could see.

I reached it and dived into it, rolling along the dusty ground. When I stopped rolling, on my belly with the Spencer muzzle thrust out in front of me, I found myself looking straight into the startled face of the second rustler. Looking too at the gaping muzzle of his rifle, pointing straight at me.

We fired almost simultaneously. I felt a sharp blow, followed by a burning sensation in my left shoulder, and I knew I had been hit.

But the rustler was also hit. On hands and knees when I had surprised him, he had come erect, still on his knees, before he was in a position to fire at me.

My bullet had caught him in the belly. There was a surprised look on his face, an unbelieving look as if this was something he had not considered. Then he doubled forward as if he had a cramp.

My trembling set in again. The sweating, which had dampened my clothes, began again. I got to my feet, my knees trembling so bad I could hardly walk. With the Spencer held at the ready, muzzle pointed at the man on the ground, I stumbled toward him. I didn't know it at the time, but I couldn't have fired again if I'd wanted to. I'd forgotten to jack another cartridge into the chamber of the gun.

But there was no need to shoot a second time. The man rolled onto his side. His open eyes stared at me accusingly.

I didn't know what to say or do. I could see the blood soaking the man's shirt from the belly wound. I could see the pain he was in by looking at his eyes and at the way his face was contorted with it.

It struck me that we couldn't continue just to look at each other. Something had to be said. I said, "I'm sorry."

The man's lips moved. I knelt, trying to make out what he said. The words weren't clear, but there could be no doubt about what he said. "The dirty sonofabitch! He said it would be easy. He said you wouldn't even have a gun."

Instantly I remembered the rattlesnake. The "he" this man was referring to had to be Rafe Joslin. It was Rafe who had sent me here today.

I said, "You're dying. What did he offer you?"

The man's eyes steadily met mine, and for a long time I thought he wasn't going to answer me. But at last he said, "Five hundred dollars. And whatever cattle we could take."

It didn't need to be said, but I said it anyway. "For killing me. Rafe Joslin offered you the money and cattle for killing me."

The man looked at me as if I was stupid. But he nodded his head. He had looked at his belly wound. He knew there was no way he could survive.

I asked, "Is there anything I can do for you? Anything I can get for you?"

He looked at the rifle I had in my hands. "You can finish me."

I couldn't continue to meet his glance. That was asking too much. I couldn't commit cold-blooded murder even to spare him the pain he was suffering. Besides that, he had no right to ask such a thing of me. He and his companion had tried to kill me. For money. Maybe I owed it to this man to make him as comfortable as possible in his last hours, but I didn't owe him more.

I asked, "Anything else?"

"There's a bottle in my saddlebags. You can bring that to me."

I stooped and picked up his rifle before I moved away. He wasn't carrying a revolver, at least none that I could see. Besides, I figured his incentive for killing me was gone. He was dying and wouldn't live to collect the money Rafe had offered for my death.

I walked back along the little gully until I came to the body of the first man I'd shot, the one with the beard. His clothes were ragged and dirty and his face was gaunt. His boots were run over at the heels and the soles of both were worn through. Cardboard showed through the holes, having been placed inside the boots to protect his feet.

I went on. Their horses were standing fifty yards away, reins trailing on the ground. Both saddles were cracked by age and weather and both were just about worn out.

I looked in the cracked saddlebags behind one of the saddles, one that bulged, and found a brown bottle half filled with whiskey. Carrying it, I went back to the wounded man. I uncorked the bottle and handed it to him.

I had no way of knowing that he had prevailed upon me to do this, not for his comfort as he lay dying, but to hasten his death. He took a long drink, his Adam's apple bobbing as he drank. Then he went into a spasm of coughing that turned his face red and made his forehead veins stand out. He dropped the bottle and fell back. I could see that he was dead.

I got to my feet. I needn't worry about the cattle. Rafe

and several members of the crew would be here tomorrow.

But I had made up my mind. I wasn't going back. Rafe Joslin was determined to kill me before I ever reached age twenty-one, maybe before I was sixteen. There were only two ways I could prevent him from eventually succeeding that I could see. One was to kill him first. The other was to run away. Nobody was going to believe my story that Rafe had hired these rustlers.

It scared me to think of leaving the only life, the only home I had ever known. I had very little money, less than five dollars in all. But I had a horse, saddle, slicker and blanket. I had the Spencer and maybe a couple of dozen rounds for it.

I didn't know whether Rafe would come after me or not. I had to assume he would, and therefore had to put as much distance between myself and the Halliday Ranch as possible.

I had a twelve-hour start, maybe twenty-four. Leaving the two dead men where they lay, their horses where they stood, I turned my horse and headed south. The wound in my shoulder hurt and made me sick at my stomach, but it wasn't a bad wound and it had bled well. There wasn't anything I could do for it, having no bandages. I'd just hope it would be all right.

Chapter IV

I held my horse to a steady, mile-eating trot. It was a gait he could maintain for hours without getting tired, and it covered a surprising amount of ground.

I'd be on Halliday land for the better part of the day, but by the time it got dark I'd be leaving it. I realized that I hadn't been off Halliday land more than half a dozen times in my entire life. The town of Halliday was surrounded by the ranch.

I thought about Rafe Joslin. I hated to leave, to give him the satisfaction of having made me run. I wondered what he'd think and what he'd do when he found the two rustlers dead. It would surprise the hell out of him, I thought, that I could have killed them both and gotten off scot-free.

What he might do about it, I couldn't guess. One possibility was that he'd take the dead bodies to the sheriff, claiming they were employees of the Halliday Ranch and that I had murdered them. Another was that he'd post me as a runaway, which would put me on the wanted list in every town for five hundred miles. If I was caught, I'd be detained until Rafe came after me. And if that happened, I'd never see home again. I'd be killed somewhere along the way back.

Still another possibility was that he'd put the ranch in

charge of one of the crew and, with Jack Standing Bear to trail, would come after me himself. That was the possibility I feared the most. I knew I couldn't hide my trail from Jack Standing Bear. Not for very long.

At sundown I began to feel hunger pangs. I was, after all, only fifteen and I had a good appetite. I hadn't brought anything to eat in my saddlebags and I knew it might be tomorrow night before I sighted a ranch house or came to a settlement or town.

I had been seeing antelope all afternoon, usually standing on a knoll from which they could see for miles. But just as the sun was going down, I came over a little rise and looked down into a dry creekbed that was lined with scrubby trees. There was a small band of antelope standing there, facing away from me. They didn't see me, because I stopped before more than my head became visible over the top of the knoll.

I dismounted immediately. I led my horse back thirty or forty feet, then crept back to the top of the knoll, crawling the last dozen yards or so.

The bunch hadn't moved. I was less than a hundred yards away, well within the Spencer's range. I got a careful bead on the largest buck in the bunch and fired.

He went down as if he'd been clubbed, hit squarely in the heart. The others were in motion before he'd hit the ground, running with their blinding speed. Before I could get up and return with my horse, they were out of sight.

Enough light remained in the sky for me to skin out one of the antelope's hindquarters. My horse didn't like the smell of blood very much, but I tied the hindquarter on behind my saddle and rode on. I didn't like wasting the rest of the meat, but I didn't have much choice. I couldn't take it all.

I wanted to stop and cook some meat and rest, but I

knew I didn't dare. Maybe when morning came I'd stop. The meat would be better then anyway. It would have cooled.

I began thinking about Rose Moran. If Rafe didn't come after me, if he stayed on Halliday Ranch, he'd try and get rid of her too. Father had left the house and land to her, but Rafe could get around that easily enough. Cattle would break down her fences and destroy her garden and flowerbeds. Fires would start in her stable, or maybe even in her house. Her horses would disappear.

Until finally she had enough of it and left. When she did, her house would be burned to the ground. Her fences would be torn out. In a couple of years, you wouldn't even be able to tell someone had once lived there.

I'd try and write to her, I thought, as soon as I reached someplace where I could mail a letter. I'd also write to Mr. Larrabee and tell him what had happened and why I'd left. He might not believe me. He might even be in cahoots with Rafe. But I didn't know that for sure.

Rafe would probably get both letters before they got to Rose or Mr. Larrabee. At least, he'd be told what the postmarks on them were. But by the time he did, I'd be a long ways from where the letters had been mailed.

I rode all night. I was tired by now, and I dozed quite a bit in the saddle. I knew there was a chance the horse would turn back toward home, so I wakened frequently to check the direction he was traveling. He kept going south, though, picking his way across the land with little or no guidance from me.

When morning came, I found a place where there were some trees near a water hole, apparently an old buffalo wallow that collected water during every rain. I broke off enough dead branches for a fire, cut some steaks off the antelope hindquarter, and fried them over the fire on sticks.

I didn't have any water and I didn't dare drink any out of the buffalo wallow. I knew I could risk getting thirsty better than I could getting sick. I'd gotten sick once from drinking out of a place such as this and I'd been in bed for a couple of days.

The antelope meat was delicious and I ate all I could hold. Then I tied what was left of the hindquarter on the saddle, mounted and headed south again.

Never before in my life had I been required to worry about how I was going to live. Halliday Ranch had been my home. I'd worked and there was food and wages and a roof over my head. Now it was going to be different. There wasn't going to be time to work, because if I stopped and worked, Rafe and Jack Standing Bear would catch up with me.

I had been riding steadily for twenty-four hours and my horse was tired. So was I. Even if Rafe and Standing Bear had left at dark when I didn't show up at home, I still had ten hours' lead on them. And I didn't see how they could have left at dark. Any undue concern on Rafe's part about my welfare would cause suspicion later when, as Rafe expected, I turned up dead. So he had probably waited through the night, only going out to find what had happened to me in the morning. If that was the case, I had a twenty-four-hour lead.

I found a bluff I could climb without taxing my horse's strength too much. I unsaddled him and rubbed his back with the saddle blanket. I tethered him with my lariat tied to a thick clump of brush, far enough back from the edge of the bluff so that he could not be seen from the plain below.

I got my slicker and blanket roll. Using them for a pillow, I laid down to sleep. Over and over again I told myself I wanted to awaken in three hours, but it was almost five when I finally did wake up.

I could tell how long I had slept from the sun's position in the sky. I hurried to the edge of the bluff and stared back along the trail I had made, looking for specks that would be horsemen, looking for the tell-tale lift of dust. I saw nothing.

The sun had started down slightly from its zenith, so I judged it must be around one o'clock. I saddled my horse. He had been grazing and seemed rested. I mounted and rode out again, still heading south.

An idea was beginning to grow in my mind. The Union Pacific Railroad ran through Cheyenne. If I kept going south, I was bound to cross the tracks. I could find my way to Cheyenne by inquiring as to which way it was from wherever I finally hit the tracks, and there I could sell my horse without running much risk that Rafe and Standing Bear would discover I had done so. They'd be trying to pick up my trail south of Cheyenne and I'd be on the train, putting miles between me and them. If I didn't buy a ticket, they couldn't find out from the ticket agent that I had taken the train, and they wouldn't have any way of knowing which way I had gone. Besides that, I'd have some money to live on for a while. I could ride one of the empty cattle or box cars and, as far as Rafe and Standing Bear were concerned, I'd just disappear.

All that day I kept my horse at a trot, but every couple of hours I'd stop and rest him for twenty minutes or so. I'd take off the saddle and cool his back by fanning it with the saddle blanket. Even so, he kept getting wearier. He showed it in the way he let his head hang down.

That night, I knew I had to stop. I'd had trouble staying awake all afternoon and my horse was very tired. I crossed a small stream as the sun was going down and took advantage of it to water my horse and to drink all I could hold myself. Here again there was a lot of scrub brush and a few

twisted and stunted trees. I tied my horse at the end of the
lariat where the feed was good and where he wouldn't get
tangled in any brush or trees. I built a small fire and cooked
some meat. I drank from the stream again, then got my
blanket roll and laid down to sleep.

I didn't even try telling myself how long I was going to
sleep. I knew it would do no good. I was too tired to
awaken before morning, but I knew the first light of dawn
would awaken me just as it always did.

As I had expected, I awoke at dawn. I got up and looked
toward where I'd tied my horse.

He was gone, and so was the lariat with which he had
been tied. Gone too was my saddle, saddle blanket, and bridle. There were boot tracks on the ground, the tracks of two
men, and a little farther away I found where two horses had
stood awhile.

It's hard to explain exactly how I felt. I was almost sick
at my stomach because I had let this happen to me. I should
have tethered the horse with one end of the lariat tied to my
wrist, so that any movement he made would have awakened
me. But I knew even that wouldn't have prevented the theft.
The thieves would simply have prevented him from pulling
against the rope.

I was angry too, but as much at myself as at the thieves. I
was also scared because it looked like now, unless the railroad tracks were close and unless Cheyenne was close to
wherever I happened onto them, Rafe and Standing Bear
were going to catch up with me. I briefly considered the
possibility that Rafe and Standing Bear had been the
thieves. I immediately discarded that idea. They couldn't
possibly have gotten this far last night and they wouldn't
have stolen my horse anyway. Rafe Joslin wanted me dead.

I followed the tracks of the three horses far enough to
find out that they weren't going south. Then I rolled up my

bed and slicker with the hindquarter of antelope inside. Fortunately I'd had the foresight to hide the Spencer under my bed, so I still had it. Carrying the rifle in one hand, the bedroll under the other arm, I started south on foot.

I'd never had much religious training except what little I'd gotten in school, but I accepted the fact that there was a God. He was supposed to look after you if you did right and punish you if you did not. I started wondering what he was punishing me for. As far as I knew, I'd always done right. Then I remembered guiltily the time Mary Jane Meier and I had sneaked away from school at lunchtime and wandered through the thick brush in the creek bottom until we were far enough away so that no one could see what we did. Mary Jane knew more about it than I did, but I sure was a willing pupil. Maybe that was what God was punishing me for right now.

Or maybe he was punishing me for killing the two rustlers. I didn't know whether I'd broken the Commandment about adultery, since neither Mary Jane nor me was married, but I sure had broken the one that said, "Thou shalt not kill." I couldn't remember anything in the Commandments that said it was all right if someone was trying to kill you, but I supposed the Lord would take that into account.

Still, I guessed it was probably unfair to blame the Lord for everything bad that happened to a person. Most folks sure didn't give Him credit for the good that happened to them. They generally took credit for that themselves.

I walked as fast as I could, but I was wearing high-heeled riding boots and they're not the most comfortable walking shoes there are. I tried to guess how many miles I could cover, walking, in a day. On horseback, even at a trot, you can cover maybe forty miles. Afoot I doubted if I was going to cover fifteen. Particularly in view of the fact that as the day wore on I was going to get more and more tired. I wasn't used to walking very much.

I couldn't help looking back every time I reached a high point of ground. I kept expecting to see Rafe and Standing Bear, or at least the tell-tale lift of dust, but I didn't see anything.

Figuring it up in my mind, I realized that I didn't have to worry about them catching up for quite a while. They'd have had to stop last night, if not to rest themselves, then to rest their mounts. The chances were good they didn't have more than one horse apiece. They probably didn't have any supplies, since Rafe had expected to find me, not the two rustlers, dead.

For a few moments I considered finding myself a good hiding place and waiting there for them. I could kill them both from ambush before they knew what was happening.

Then I remembered the sick feeling I'd had after killing the two rustlers, and I knew that when the showdown came I'd never be able to pull the trigger, either against Standing Bear or Rafe. Maybe the Lord would forgive someone for killing to defend his life. He sure wouldn't forgive two killings in cold blood.

So I kept walking. The wind blew constantly, but it was a warm wind as soon as the morning chill wore off. I kept looking ahead. Once I thought I saw a faint layer of smoke, but with the wind blowing like it was, it was difficult to tell.

Finally, from the top of a knoll, I saw a wooden water tower and a windmill in the distance ahead of me with some small, scattered buildings at its base. I broke into a run, but I stopped running after less than a hundred yards. Water tower and buildings were still a mile away, and I couldn't run that far.

The water tower and windmill meant the railroad tracks.

The smoke I thought I'd seen earlier must have come from a locomotive.

From half a mile, I could see that the buildings at the base of the water tower were some kind of station. I saw clothes flapping on a clothesline, and once I saw a man walk between two of the buildings. Several horses were in a corral.

I stopped long enough to think it out. Tomorrow, Rafe and Standing Bear would follow my trail straight to the railroad track. They would have read the tracks back at my last night's camp and would know exactly what had happened to me. My boot tracks would be as easily followed as my horse's tracks had been earlier.

They'd follow to the railroad tracks and they'd believe I had gone no farther. But they'd have no idea which way I'd gone unless I let those people at that station see me and talk to me. They wouldn't even know whether I'd caught a train or whether I had chosen to walk along the tracks. Stepping on the ties, I wouldn't leave a trail that even someone as expert as Standing Bear could follow.

So they'd have to check out four possibilities. That I'd caught the train, heading either east or west. That I'd walked along the tracks, either east or west. Or maybe a fifth possibility, that I'd been picked up by a wagon or buckboard at some place where a road happened to cross the tracks.

I made a big circle to the east, staying in gullies and behind low hills so that I wouldn't be spotted by anybody at the ramshackle railroad station ahead of me. And at last I reached the tracks and sat down to rest and try and decide what I was going to do.

Chapter V

I was hungry, but I didn't want to build a fire because I was afraid the smoke from it would be seen by somebody at the railroad station. Rafe and Standing Bear would trail me to this spot, but they wouldn't know which way I had gone from here.

I hadn't yet made up my mind what I wanted to do. I guessed it didn't really matter. I'd probably try to get on the first train that came by on these tracks, eastbound or westbound. Anything to get me away quickly before Rafe and Standing Bear arrived.

I rested awhile and then I got up and walked along the ties back toward the water tower, which I could see plainly from where I was. I had gone less than a quarter mile before I heard a faint whistle from behind and, turning, saw a faint puff of black smoke in the distance. It was an approaching train and it was headed west.

There was no way I could know how long it was. What I did know was that I hadn't much chance of catching it unless it either slowed considerably or stopped.

The engine would probably stop at the water tower, and that would leave the rest of the train strung out on the east side of the station.

I began to run, taking care to step only on the creosoted

ties. They weren't spaced right for easy walking or running, but I managed to adjust my gait so that I stepped on every other one. The train whistled again behind me, closer this time. Glancing back, I could see it, now a quarter mile away.

I was still nearly a quarter mile from the water tower. I speeded up as much as I could. Once, my boots tripped me and I sprawled on the cinder-covered roadbed. I got up immediately, my hands and knees scratched, and kept running as if my life depended on it.

The engine whistled again, getting very close. I left the railroad tracks and dived for a thick clump of sagebrush nearby. I rolled, and came to rest beside the clump of brush, still clutching my bedroll and my Spencer rifle. The engine came abreast of me.

It was the first train I had ever seen. Its noise was terrifying. Looking up, I saw a man in a striped cap leaning from the window at the rear of the engine. He had seen me and was watching me. He didn't wave.

Then the cars were rattling past. When the last one, the caboose, went by, I got up and began to run. If there was anybody in the caboose, they must have been looking out the other side, because I didn't see anyone.

The train stopped as I came even with the caboose. I ran on until I reached a boxcar with a door that was partway open. I forced it open a little wider and climbed inside, after first throwing my rifle and bedroll in.

Immediately I turned around and closed the door. It was nearly pitch-black inside the car. I realized uneasily that Rafe and Standing Bear might pick up my trail for the short distance I'd run beside the tracks. If they did, they'd know I had gone west. Maybe it would be smart of me to get off this train a few miles west of the water tower and catch one heading east. Or maybe, if I just stayed on this train I would be safe. I didn't see how they could possibly know where I had gotten off, and they couldn't ride the tracks for a couple of hundred miles trying to pick up my trail.

For the first time since my encounter with the rustlers, I began to feel a little hope. I felt my way along the wall of the dark interior of the boxcar until I came to the corner. I sat down on my bedroll, holding the rifle upright between my knees.

The train was stopped for fifteen or twenty minutes. Taking on water, I supposed. Once, I thought I heard someone breathing inside the boxcar. I listened intently, with chills running along my spine, but I didn't hear it again and I decided I had imagined it.

Finally, the train started with a jerk. I could hear the couplings between the cars successively as the train's forward movement took up the slack. The car I was in jerked into motion and rolled along the track noisily, gradually picking up speed.

When I thought we had left the water tower and buildings behind, I got up and felt my way along the wall to the door. I didn't like sitting in the dark. I opened the door, having to put down my rifle and bedroll in order to exert the necessary strength.

It opened about a foot, letting in the light. I stooped to recover my Spencer and bedroll.

Something hit me, hard, and sent me reeling across the car. I fell, unable to keep my feet, and felt the splinters from the worn, uneven floor, penetrate my hands and knees. I wasn't hurt, though, and I stared back at the partly open door.

There were two men there. One had picked up my Spencer and was examining it. The other had my bedroll. He was on his knees opening it. He found the part hindquarter of antelope and held it up triumphantly.

Both men wore beards. Both had long, unkempt hair and both were incredibly dirty. I got up and walked toward them. I said, "Give me that rifle and bedroll. They're mine."

The man with my rifle laughed. "You hear the kid, Sime? He says this stuff is his. Why don't you give it back?"

I felt like a fool. I'd climbed into this boxcar without even considering the possibility that it might have other occupants. I'd even heard one of them breathing, but I'd convinced myself I was imagining things. Now they had my gun and bedroll and they sure as hell weren't going to give them back. I'd be lucky if I got out of this alive.

The train was now moving along at a good pace. It swayed from side to side, but neither of the two men seemed to have any trouble keeping their balance.

The Spencer was pointing straight at me. I'd heard the man jack a cartridge into the chamber earlier, and I wondered if he was going to murder me in cold blood and throw my body out of the car.

In the light coming through the partly open door, I could see his eyes. They were cold, narrowed, almost green. There were tobacco stains on the beard below his mouth and on his mustache above it.

I couldn't seem to speak. I tried to get some words out, but I only croaked. I remembered that rattlesnake striking out at me and I remembered I'd saved myself by pushing myself backward out of his reach.

Cautiously, slowly so as not to startle the man with the rifle, I got to my feet. I rubbed my splinter-filled hands on the sides of my pants.

The man with the bedroll said, "Go ahead, Red. Shoot him. If you don't, he'll have the law waitin' for us at the next station."

I suddenly remembered seeing poles with wires on them running beside the tracks. Telegraph wires. They knew that, if they let me live, I could walk back to the station where the train had stopped for water and telegraph ahead.

Sime said, "The caboose is only two cars back. Somebody might hear the shot."

"Then hit him with the goddam thing and we'll throw him out."

"Maybe he's got somethin' else on him. Money or a pocketknife."

Red looked at me. He had been sitting comfortably on my bedroll with his back to the boxcar wall. Now he got to his feet. The pair separated and came at me from two sides. Sime had the rifle held like a club, but not by the barrel. He held it by the stock, apparently intending to hit me with the heavy barrel.

I backed straight away from them. I didn't want to let them corner me. I had about five dollars and I had a pocketknife, but I wasn't about to give up my life defending them. Besides, if I took out the money and the pocketknife, it might divert them long enough for me to get away.

The only way to escape from them was through that partly open door, an opening hardly more than a foot wide. The fall might kill me, but if I stayed here Sime and Red were going to kill me anyway.

I didn't have to make my voice sound scared. It sounded that way naturally. I said, "I got five dollars and a knife. You let me go and I'll give them to you."

Sime laughed that nasty laugh again. With hands that shook almost uncontrollably, I fished in my pocket. I brought out a handful, three silver dollars and a lot of change. The knife was in the other pocket. I started to shift the money from one hand to the other, but before I could, I realized they were too close. There wasn't time. Sime was already drawing the rifle back to strike.

I dropped the money, making it look like I hadn't intended to. For just an instant, the eyes of both men went from me to the money rolling on the boxcar floor.

I didn't hesitate. I sprinted between them straight for the narrow opening in the door, knowing I'd have to turn myself sideways to get through.

As I passed him, Sime recovered and swung the rifle savagely. It hit me across the back, giving further impetus to my dive for the open door. At the same time, Red stuck out his foot and tripped me.

I reached the door sliding on the splintery floor. My back was numb from the blow of the rifle barrel, but I didn't even notice the splinters in my hands and knees. I got my hands on the sides of the partly open door and with all the strength of which I was capable, propelled myself on through. I almost made it. I thought I was clear, then I felt one of my boots grabbed and I was left hanging, my head missing the sharp corners of the railroad ties by less than an inch.

Either the man who held my boot couldn't hold on or else he thought the fall would kill me. It must have been obvious to him that when I fell my head would hit the ties. He let go and I fell.

I felt a sharp blow on the side of my head, felt my neck wrenched violently, and then I was rolling end over end down the steep cinder embankment and into the brush that lined the tracks. I stayed conscious until I stopped rolling. Then, with my head aching violently and burning over nearly every inch of my body, everything went black.

It was dark when I awakened. I was lying on my stomach and my first thought was that I was dead. Then I felt the incredible pain in my head and neck and all the gravel and cinder-filled abrasions on my body and I knew I was alive.

I remembered what had happened to me. I'd had another

close brush with death. I broke into a sweat thinking about how close it had really been.

I rolled over and tried to sit up, but my head began throbbing so mercilessly I had to fall back again. Maybe it would have been better if I had been killed, I thought.

Lying there, I remembered that Rafe and Standing Bear were still trailing me. If they caught me, regardless of the condition I was in, they'd either kill me outright or take me back to face murder charges in the death of the two rustlers. If Standing Bear balked at my murder, Rafe would likely kill him too.

And they'd be coming, maybe as early as tomorrow. But for the moment I was safe, hidden by darkness. I had time to plan.

My head ached so terribly it was hard to think. I put up an exploring hand and discovered a bad bump on my right temple that had bled freely. The blood was clotted all over my forehead and the side of my face. It was even in my ear.

My rifle was gone. So was my bedroll and so was the antelope meat. My money was gone. All I had was a pocketknife. For a few moments I considered walking back to the railroad water stop and asking help from whoever was there.

I discarded that idea immediately. Nobody was going to believe a fifteen-year-old boy. Nobody was going to take my word against Rafe's and that of Standing Bear. I'd simply be turned over to them when they arrived. Chances were I'd never get back to Halliday Ranch alive.

But the more I thought about it, the more hopeful I became. Faced with my disappearance into thin air at the water stop, Rafe would have to decide in which direction he ought to look for me.

He could probably find out that the only train last night had been westbound. But he'd still have to check out the chance that I had walked east, staying on the ties so as to leave no trail. He might send Standing Bear east, knowing that if there was a trail, Standing Bear would find some trace of it before he had gone a dozen miles.

That was going to take time, at least until noon, assuming Rafe and Standing Bear arrived at the water stop sometime during the night.

Having ruled out the possibility that I had gone east, they would want to rule out the chance that I had kept going south. That would take less time. Standing Bear could simply make a circle of the settlement looking for my tracks.

Having checked out those two possibilities, Rafe would know I had gone west, either aboard the train or walking on the ties. He would telegraph ahead, asking law officers in the next town to search the train for me. Chances were good he and Standing Bear would then come riding along the track, searching for any little mistake I might have made.

That gave me a respite at least until noon tomorrow. I'd wait for daybreak. Then I'd take a look at the embankment I'd rolled down last night. I'd do what I could to hide the marks I'd made. After that, I'd try to find someplace where I could hide myself, being as careful as I could to leave nothing Standing Bear might see.

The thought of trying to outwit such an expert tracker as Standing Bear scared the hell out of me. I didn't see how I could do it, but I had no other choice than to try. Not until they had gone on past this place would I be free to leave.

One thing was in my favor. Standing Bear was going to be scrutinizing the ties and the cinders between the ties. By the time he got to this place, he would have been trailing a lot of miles, a dozen or so going east, maybe a dozen or so along the tracks going west. He would not be as alert as he might have been earlier.

I rested, keeping my head still so that it wouldn't ache so terribly, waiting for the dawn. I didn't dare go to sleep for fear I would sleep too long and wake up with Rafe and Standing Bear looking down at me. The time dragged endlessly. But at last, gray began to streak the sky.

I remained motionless until it was light enough to see for half a mile. Then I sat up, removed my boots and got carefully to my feet.

Between me and the railroad tracks there were only cinders and coarse crushed rock. The path I had rolled down was almost impossible to see. Furthermore, Standing Bear wasn't going to be looking for the imprint made by a body rolling down the embankment. He was going to be looking for tracks. I figured I could forget about trying to hide the marks I'd made after I fell from the car.

But the imprint of my body here and the tracks I made leaving were something else. Standing in my stocking feet, I stared away from the tracks, looking for a place where I could hide.

The only thing I could see was a pile of brush and dry grass that had been cut from along the right-of-way so that sparks from the engine wouldn't start a prairie fire. It wasn't big enough to hide behind, but if I pulled it over me . . .

Looking around, I saw a loose branch of sagebrush that had been missed by the railroad clean-up crew. I picked it up.

With my boots in one hand, the branch in the other, I backed toward the pile of brush and grass, brushing out the tracks made unavoidably by my stocking feet.

Standing Bear would find my trail easily enough if he happened to be watching carefully for it. What I was hoping was that he'd be intent on the ground directly between the two railroad tracks. Just a moment's inattention on his part and he'd go past this place without noticing anything unusual. Once he and Rafe had passed I'd be safe. At least for a while.

Chapter VI

When I reached the pile of brush and grass, I looked carefully all around to make sure I wasn't being observed. The horizons were empty on all sides for as far as I could see.

From right beside it, the pile looked awfully skimpy to hide anything. But it was all there was and I'd have to make it do. I began separating it into two long, equal piles, and when I had done that, I sat down on the ground between them. I covered my feet and legs, then my body. I arranged a pile of what was left so that I could pull it over my head when I saw them coming along the tracks.

Having done all I could, I made myself relax. I thought back on all the things that had happened to me and decided I hadn't been very smart. Having Rafe after me was bad enough, but if I wasn't smarter in the future than I had been in the past, Rafe wasn't going to get a chance at me. Someone else was sure to get me first.

I'd started out with a horse, a rifle and a little money. Now all I had left was a pocketknife and the clothes on my back.

Strangely enough, thinking of all that had happened to me didn't discourage me. It only made me mad. The sun finally went down and dusk crept across the land. When it was fully dark, I closed my eyes and tried to sleep. My shoulder ached from the bullet wound. It had opened up and bled when I rolled down the embankment and I was bruised and sore all over.

It was summer, but in Wyoming the wind always blows, and at night and in early morning it's cool even in the summertime. I was grateful for the brush and grass with which I'd covered myself because it helped to keep me warm. I either passed out or went to sleep.

Several times I awakened. Once, a train went past, heading east. Another time I was wakened with a sharp thorn sticking into my neck.

I awakened for the last time when the sun was halfway up the sky. I raised my head enough to look around. I didn't see anything.

I felt a little foolish lying there covered with brush and grass. I didn't know for sure that Rafe and Standing Bear would be coming this way looking for me. But I did know I'd made all the mistakes I could afford. If the Lord hadn't been looking out for me, I'd have been dead a long time ago. The snake could have bitten me in the face or neck. The rustlers could have killed me if I hadn't dived from the saddle exactly when I had. The two who had stolen my horse and saddle could have murdered me in my sleep. And finally, the two in the boxcar had intended to kill me and they had tried.

Rafe and Standing Bear had to be coming this way in the next few hours, I told myself. Only when they had gone past would I dare leave my hiding place.

The sun crawled slowly across the sky. My brush shelter began to get hot. I sweated and the sweat just made the places where the skin had been scratched burn and itch. I wanted to scratch fifty times an hour, but whenever I did, I forced myself to think of something else.

The grating sound of something coming along the cinder

railroad bed almost took me by surprise. I didn't raise my head to look. I just pulled the pile of brush and grass I had previously prepared over my face and then wriggled my arms down until they, too, were out of sight.

The brush and grass over my face didn't entirely shut out the light, and I discovered that if I opened my eyes I could see. Not everything and not very well, but I could see well enough to distinguish objects. A shadow fell across the brush under which I was hiding and I held my breath. The grating I had heard was that of horses' hoofs and, peering through the brush covering, I saw two horses. One was between the rails. The other was between me and the rails.

I could only dimly see the rider nearest me, but the horse was Rafe's all right. Shiny black he was, with white stockings on his front feet, with a white blaze on his face. Recognizing the horse, I didn't have to see who was riding him. Nor did I have to see who it was between the tracks.

My lungs were bursting from holding my breath. The sounds of hoofs grating in the gravel and cinders that made up the roadbed diminished gradually. Only when they had faded entirely did I dare let my breath sigh slowly out. I lay there, breathing shallowly for a long time, but finally I dared to raise my head and look westward along the track.

Rafe Joslin and Standing Bear were nearly a quarter mile away. But they were unmistakable. Standing Bear was a Sioux and was so tall and broad across the shoulders that he seemed to dwarf the horse. Rafe was short and skinny and equally unmistakable.

I knew I didn't dare get up yet. There was still a chance one of them would turn his head and look back, or that they would decide I had gone some other way and come riding back.

I watched them until they were out of sight more than a mile away where the railroad tracks disappeared into a cut through a shallow knoll. Then I got up carefully and, standing in gravel, I restored the pile of brush to as near its original state as I could.

Carrying my boots, I walked carefully away from the railroad tracks for a couple of hundred yards, stepping on rocks or on clumps of bunch grass so that I would leave no tracks. Only when I was a quarter of a mile south of the tracks did I stop, sit down, and pull on my boots.

I was thirsty and I was ravenously hungry. I still hurt all over when I moved, but the abrasions I'd gotten falling from the boxcar had scabbed over and didn't burn the way they had at first. The shoulder wound had stopped bleeding again. It had hurt when the fall reopened it, but having it reopen had probably been good for it. Bleeding tended to carry dirt and infection from a wound, and this one was deep enough to give me a lot of trouble if infection ever got into it.

Now, I asked myself, what the hell was I going to do? I hadn't a dime. I hadn't a weapon with which to kill myself some game. I hadn't a horse. I was hungry and thirsty, and south of the railroad tracks it was probably at least fifty miles to the nearest settlement. Furthermore, I didn't dare show my face to anyone. Rafe would have telegraphed every settlement for a couple of hundred miles.

Furthermore, he and Standing Bear would likely be returning along the tracks sometime before dark tonight to see if any reply had come to their telegrams.

I wondered if Standing Bear knew why Rafe was pursuing me so relentlessly. Standing Bear might be in it with Rafe. He too might kill me if he got the chance. But I doubted it. Standing Bear had no reason for hating me and nothing to gain by my death. I doubted if Rafe could have bought Standing Bear's loyalty by promising to pay him if they succeeded in finding and killing me.

I decided that food and water were a necessity if I was going to survive. And since I couldn't let myself be seen, that left only one alternative. Stealing it.

With my mind made up, I headed back toward the water tower and the few buildings at the foot of it. I was tired and weak, and I hurt from head to toe. My shoulder was especially sore.

For a few moments I considered letting Rafe find me, counting on Standing Bear's loyalty to my father to keep him from letting Rafe murder me. But Rafe wouldn't let Standing Bear prevent him from killing me. If Standing Bear objected, Rafe would simply kill him too.

As far as I was from the railroad tracks, I didn't think there was much chance Standing Bear could find my trail on his way back to the water tower.

I trudged along wearily until I was within four or five hundred yards of the place. Then I found myself a place to hide behind a thick clump of brush. I'd have to wait for dark, but I could see the railroad track from here and I'd know when Rafe and Standing Bear came back.

A faint whistle and a puff of black smoke on the eastern horizon warned of the approach of a train. This was the daily westbound I'd boarded yesterday with such disastrous results. I saw it stop in the settlement long enough to take on water. Then it chugged out of the station, gradually picking up speed. Too late, I realized it might have been a good idea if I'd worked my way around east of the water tower and taken today's westbound. Neither Rafe nor Standing Bear would have expected me to be on it.

The train puffed steadily west and finally went out of sight. I remained hidden. Rafe and Standing Bear would stay at the settlement tonight, I thought. But what would they do tomorrow? They had lost my trail. Well, for one thing, in the morning they'd circle the settlement, again carefully looking for my trail. If they didn't find it, the chances were good that they'd take the train west tomorrow, since the eastbound had gone by too early yesterday for me to have boarded it.

If they did, that would give me a little freedom of movement, at least temporarily. I could head south again, and by the time they realized I had not gone west and had come back, my trail should be wiped out by the everlasting wind.

I'd just have to ignore my hunger and thirst until they left tomorrow, no matter how difficult it was. If I didn't, I'd leave a trail going into the settlement and leaving it that Standing Bear was sure to find.

Knowing it would pass the time more quickly, I closed my eyes and tried to sleep. My shoulder still was sore, and so were the abrasions on my body. I worried a little about their becoming infected, but there was nothing I could do about it, so I finally went to sleep. I awakened near sundown, in time to see Rafe and Standing Bear returning to the settlement along the tracks. I felt relieved that they had not picked up my trail where I'd dived off the train. They disappeared among the buildings of the settlement.

Shortly thereafter, while there was still light in the sky, I saw Standing Bear making a big circle of the settlement, his eyes on the ground. It was nearly dark when he finished. The last light faded from the sky, and a few lamps winked from the windows of the buildings clustered beneath the water tower.

I knew it was foolish, but I couldn't wait. My mouth was so parched and dry that I could scarcely swallow any more. My stomach was cramping with hunger. As soon as it was completely dark, I got to my feet and headed toward the settlement.

Maybe I'd get caught. But by now my thirst and hunger were such that I really didn't care. And if I did not get caught, I might be able to obtain a horse as well as food and water.

Slowly and cautiously I worked my way toward the settlement. One of the buildings was larger than the others and also had more lights in it. Peering in the window from a distance, I saw several men, including Rafe and Standing Bear, sitting at a long table with benches on either side. A dark-faced Mexican woman was serving them.

I went on by, straight to the water tower. The windmill was turning briskly in the wind. It pumped water to the tower, I thought. A leaky pipe dripped a steady stream of water onto the ground between the two. I got under it and drank until I couldn't hold any more.

Food was something else. But there ought to be a root cellar someplace nearby, and there might be meat hanging on the back porch of the building where all the men were eating now.

Hurrying, because I knew they wouldn't stay at the table forever, I found the root cellar and went down into it, taking care that I closed the door silently. It smelled musty and damp and I didn't have any light. I felt around until I located some potatoes and a gunnysack. I put a couple of dozen potatoes into it and went back up the steps.

There was a porch in back of the building where I'd seen the men eating. Carefully, I opened the screen door. The wooden floor creaked thunderously, but I found a slab of bacon hanging and took it down off its hook. There were several others, so I doubted if it would be missed.

I went back outside and found my potato sack. I put the bacon into it.

The temptation to try and find a weapon was overpowering, as was the temptation to steal myself a horse. But I knew that if I did either one, weapon and horse would be missed. When they were, Standing Bear would scout the ground for tracks again. He'd find mine and the chase would be on again.

I doubted if the potatoes and bacon would be missed. If I left with only them, chances were nobody would follow me. I needed matches, though, so I went to the corral where half a dozen saddles were visible on the top rail, and fumbled in several saddlebags until I found a handful of them. Then, with the gunnysack over my shoulder, the matches in my pocket, I headed south, afoot.

The lights faded behind me until they were no longer visible. But the stars were bright enough for me to see the ground.

I walked for six or seven hours at a steady if not a brisk pace. I'd slept a lot both last night and earlier today. Furthermore, the walking tended to reduce the soreness both in my shoulder and in my body where the skin had been scraped off.

There was no way I could tell whether I'd gotten away or not. Standing Bear had scouted a circle around the settlement before it got dark yesterday. He had scouted the railroad tracks going west without finding the place I had rolled down the embankment off the train.

He wasn't likely to search for my tracks in either place again. That meant they'd figure I had left the settlement aboard the train.

They'd likely wait now to hear from stations west of here in reply to their telegrams. If they telegraphed east, they'd wait for answers from there too.

What they'd do when they got negative responses from both directions I couldn't guess. Maybe they'd give up and go back home. But I wasn't willing to bet on it.

The chances were, Standing Bear would make another, more careful circle of the settlement. When he did, he'd find my tracks. And he and Rafe would be on my trail again.

Chapter VII

Once more I was fleeing, with only the night between me and my pursuers. The difference was that before I'd had a horse and gun. Now I was afoot with nothing but a pocket-knife, some potatoes, and a slab of bacon. Furthermore, I'd walked so much that the soles of my boots were beginning to wear through. Maybe, I thought, when I stopped at dawn I could cut insoles from the bacon rind. They ought to last awhile.

I guided myself by the evening star, which hung low above the horizon in the west. It set eventually, but by then I had another star by which to guide myself. Sometimes I fell because I couldn't see the ground. But I kept going until dawn began to streak the eastern sky.

I thought about Rose Moran. She must know that Rafe was pursuing me and she would know instinctively what he intended to do to me when he caught up. I had a brief and forlorn hope that maybe she could alert the sheriff and that he would telegraph to other sheriffs' offices. Then I decided it wasn't going to happen. Rose had been my father's woman, not his wife. Nothing she said would carry much weight with the sheriff in Halliday.

I still had not faced, in my own mind, how I was going to get out of this, provided it was possible. Was I prepared to shoot Rafe Joslin to save my own life? Was I certain enough that he meant to kill me that I could commit murder myself?

I shook my head slightly. I didn't think I could kill Rafe unless I were actually looking down the barrel of his gun. And by then it would be too late.

Standing Bear was no different. I felt sure he didn't know what Rafe meant to do to me. Which would make it impossible for me to kill Standing Bear under any circumstances.

So deep was I in my own thoughts that I didn't see the thin plume of smoke rising from a shallow creekbed ahead of me. By the time I did see it, it was too late. There was a camp in the creekbed. There were seven horses. And there were seven men, three squatted around the fire, four others in the act of bringing horses in and readying them for the day.

So far as I was concerned, there was only one thing wrong. The seven were Indians. Cheyennes, I thought, judging from what beadwork they were wearing.

I whirled instantly, but their guns came up, and those who didn't have guns snatched up their sinew-backed bows and fitted arrows to the strings.

I stopped. Running would only get me shot in the back. I dropped the gunnysack and extended my hands away from my body, palms toward the men and fingers spread. Like I was talking to a nervous horse I said, "Easy now. I ain't even got a gun."

The oldest didn't look more than thirty, and the youngest was about my age. The oldest, who seemed to be in charge, gave an order to a couple of the others. They came toward me, guns ready. I made it a point to stand absolutely still. One rammed his rifle into my belly while the other picked up the gunnysack and looked inside. He said something and tossed the sack toward the fire.

The older Indian spoke again and the one with the gun in my belly backed away. The Indian leader beckoned me. I walked slowly toward him. He tried talking to me in the Cheyenne tongue and by the inflection of his voice I knew he was questioning me. But I couldn't understand.

Finally I pointed to myself. Then I ran in place for several seconds. Then I pointed in the direction I had come and made a gesture like a man raising a gun to his shoulder. I staggered away, then pulled back my bloodstained shirt and showed the Indians my shoulder wound.

I could see immediately that my sign language had been understood. I'd stretched the truth a little by letting on that Rafe had shot me, but these Indians wouldn't know the difference, and it had been important that I make them understand.

After that they seemed to lose interest in me. They finished readying their horses. They had no camp gear. There was the leg bone of an antelope lying thirty or forty feet from camp where someone had thrown it, but there wasn't any meat on it. I expected they'd take my gunnysack of food, but they didn't even look at it.

When they all were ready, they mounted their horses by leaping easily to their backs. I felt a vast relief. They were going to leave without killing me or without even stealing the food I had.

When they all were mounted, the older one said something. The youngest, the one that looked about my age, beckoned and then pointed to the horse's back directly behind him. I understood he meant me to get on the horse in back of him.

I shook my head. The older Indian shrugged just like a white man might have done, then led out toward the southeast, the others following along behind. None of them looked back.

It didn't take but an instant for this to register in my thoughts. They meant me no harm. They were even willing to help me escape from whoever was chasing me. But if I didn't want to go, it made no difference to them.

I yelled, "Wait!"

The one in the lead stopped his horse and looked around. I picked up my gunnysack and ran after them. I handed it up to the young Indian. He reached down a hand to help me up, and I vaulted up behind him. Without saying anything or looking at me again, the older Indian led out a second time, with the others following. They traveled according to age, I guessed, because the one I was riding with came last.

I'd been going to eat as soon as it got light enough to find some firewood. I hadn't had the chance. But I'd had all the water I wanted last night, and if you have water you can go a long time without food.

Of two things I was fairly sure. The Indians, by letting me go with them, had probably saved my life. Rafe and Standing Bear would have caught up with me before noon.

The second was that the Indians meant me no harm. Otherwise they wouldn't have given me the choice of going with them or staying behind. I thought that maybe, if they went to their village, my trail would be lost in a couple of hundred other trails. Maybe I could obtain a horse and get clear away.

For now, I was sleepy and my whole body hurt. Balancing myself on the Indian's horse's rump, I dozed, each time awakening only when my head began to loll to one side or the other.

The seven Indians were in no apparent hurry. They traveled with their horses at a walk. All were alert, watching the horizons and staying in low-lying ground so that they could not be seen from very far away. They also kept a careful watch on the ground for tracks.

They were hunting, I supposed. I thought about the bacon and potatoes in my gunnysack and wished we could stop, build a fire and eat. I made myself think of something else. What I found myself thinking about was what was likely to happen if Rafe and Standing Bear caught up with these Indians.

Both Rafe and Standing Bear had repeating Spencers and probably revolvers as well. By contrast, only four of the Indians had guns, and these were the old trapdoor Springfields, single shot. The others had sinew-backed bows and arrows.

Well, I thought, if it came to a fight between Rafe and Standing Bear and the Indians, I'd just have to give myself up to Rafe. The Indians had helped me and I wasn't going to let them get slaughtered because of me.

We traveled at a steady walk in a southeasterly direction for about six hours before the Indians came to a wide, sandy streambed with a trickle of water in the middle. For half a mile on each side of the sandy streambed there were trees and grass and brush. All dismounted except the one behind whom I was riding. He motioned for me to dismount, and when I had, drove the other ponies into the trees so that they could graze.

The Indians built a fire, paying no attention to me. I put my gunnysack down beside the fire and went after firewood. I figured I could pull my own weight with Indians or anybody else.

When the fire was going well, the Indians got out some dried meat and began to chew on it. I knew what it was. Pemmican was the Indian name. Jerky was what the white men called it, except that pemmican had dried berries mixed with it. It was nourishing enough and didn't taste bad, but it was hard to chew. I dug in the sack, got out the bacon and cut the rind off it. I cut the rest into pieces and then gestured to the Indians to help themselves. While they were doing it, I took off my boots, drew a pattern on the bacon rind with a stick, then began cutting insoles for myself.

The Indians were cooking the bacon on sticks over the fire. The grease dripped into it, sending up a pretty noticeable column of smoke. I finished with the insoles and cooked myself a piece of bacon, which I ate half raw. When I had finished, I walked to where the young Indian was watching the horses and made signs to indicate I would take over his job.

He looked at me doubtfully, wanting to go to the fire but not altogether trusting me. Finally the older Indian called to him from the fire. He left me there with the horses, afoot, and rode his own horse back to the fire. I didn't blame them for being cautious. Their experiences with white men had probably not inspired much trust in them.

They lolled around the fire for nearly an hour. I understood that they were resting their horses as much as they were themselves. Then they all came and caught their horses. They mounted and the boy my age motioned for me to mount behind him. I handed up my sack of potatoes and then vaulted to the horse's back behind him. We rode out, still on the same southeasterly course.

I felt sure that Rafe had, by now, cut the trail of the Indians. I wondered what he thought. Probably that they had kidnaped me. Then I shook my head. Standing Bear was expert at reading trail. He would find no signs of struggle. He would find instead where I had run after the Indians. Standing Bear would know I had gone with the Indians of my own free will.

We traveled at a steady walk for a good part of the afternoon. At last the older Indian stopped. The others caught up with him and they all sat their horses several moments studying the ground.

The trail that interested them was that of a number of buffalo. Guessing, I'd have said maybe twenty or thirty of them, ranging from huge old bulls to calves.

The Indians talked among themselves for several minutes. I couldn't understand their words but I knew they were talking about the trail, guessing how old it was and what their chances were of overtaking the herd before it got dark tonight. Finally they turned into the buffalo trail, urging their horses to a trot.

It was harder for me to balance myself on the horse's rump at a trot than it had been at a walk, but I was determined not to hold onto the Indian boy. There was no danger now that I would doze off. Besides, I was as eager about catching up with the buffalo as the Indians were. I decided they probably wouldn't kill more than two. They wouldn't be able to take more than two back to their village, wherever that was, and Indians never killed more game than they could use.

It was midafternoon when we finally came over a long ridge and looked down into a wide valley. The Indian leading us stopped immediately. The others came up beside him and all of us stared at the scene below.

There had been more than thirty buffalo in the herd. I counted forty-one skinned carcasses lying scattered in that shallow valley. They must have been killed and skinned yesterday because some of them were already beginning to bloat. As we approached, forty or fifty buzzards rose from their perches on the carcasses. Half a dozen wolves kept their distance from us, finally disappearing over the next ridge. Several coyotes were bolder, being satisfied to stay at a distance of about a hundred and fifty yards.

The face of the Indian leader was like a thundercloud. He looked at me as if he hated me, and for a moment I thought I was going to be killed. They talked among themselves, and if their words weren't understandable, their tones sure were. They were furious, and rightly so, I thought. They had wanted a couple of buffalo and had ridden for days looking for them. They would have taken meat, hides and parts of the entrails back to their village where every morsel would have been used.

But white hunters didn't work that way. They killed everything they found and they took only the hides, leaving the rest to rot. At the conclusion of their discussion, the boy behind whom I was riding pushed me roughly from the horse. I stumbled, but I managed to keep my feet.

One of the Indians raised a gun, sighted it on my chest and pulled the hammer back. I was too frozen with fear to think. I knew that in another instant a bullet was going to smash into me.

The older Indian spoke sharply. The man with the gun glanced at him rebelliously. The leader spoke again. Finally, reluctantly, the Indian with the gun lowered it.

I was sweating now and my knees were trembling. Suddenly, with no more than a brief command from their leader, the Indians turned from me and rode slowly away, following the twin tracks of the wagon in which the hunters had hauled away the hides.

I was left alone, with my sack of potatoes. The buzzards began circling lower and the wolves reappeared over the crest of the ridge. I wondered if any of the buffalo meat would still be edible. I went to one of the carcasses and cut a small piece off the hump with my pocketknife. I smelled it and it smelled all right, so I cut a bigger piece and dropped it into the gunnysack. No use taking more than I could eat today, because by tomorrow it would be spoiled.

I hesitated about which way I ought to go. There were a lot of boot tracks here and I thought maybe I could throw Standing Bear off and make him think I was still with the Indians. Scuffing my boots as I walked, I went to the carcass at the far edge of the group. Here I sat on the dried rump of the skinned buffalo and removed my boots. Carrying them and the gunnysack, I stepped from clump to clump of the buffalo grass that covered the ground. Each time I did, I crushed its curly blades, but if Standing Bear thought I was still with the Indians he probably wouldn't check things like that too close.

I traveled this way for nearly three hundred yards. Then I sat down and put my boots back on.

I suppose it would have been smarter of me to head straight east and put both Indians and the two pursuing me a long ways behind. The reason I didn't was that I wasn't equipped either to travel far or to survive for very long.

So I headed south in the same direction buffalo hunters and Indians had gone. The buffalo hunters had to have a camp close by. I didn't like the idea of stealing a horse very much, but if survival depended on it I was prepared to put my scruples aside.

Night caught up with me before I sighted anything, either smoke or camp, or the trail of either Indians or the hunters they were following.

I was tired and didn't feel like walking any more. I wished I had my blanket roll but I didn't so I found myself a place in a dry wash where the wind didn't hit me. I was too tired to build a fire and I'd had some bacon at noon, so I didn't think it would hurt me to go hungry tonight. If the buffalo meat spoiled, then I'd just have to throw it away. I did get it out, though, and laid it on a flat rock so it would have a chance to dry.

I had hardly more than lain down before I was asleep.

Chapter VIII

I had very little that was worth stealing. Nevertheless, while I was sleeping some night-hunting animal had taken the buffalo meat I had so carefully laid out on a rock to dry.

By now I was so hungry that I knew I had to eat something or I wouldn't be able to travel any more. I gathered dry branches of brush along with a few dry buffalo chips. I laid the fire carefully so I wouldn't use more than one match lighting it. When it was ready, I struck the match and touched it to the pile. It caught immediately and, fanned by the breeze, grew rapidly.

Buffalo chips make a practically smokeless fire. While it blazed up, I peeled one of the potatoes and cut it into slices so that it would cook more quickly. Then, after breaking off a number of long, straight branches from nearby brush clumps, I speared slivers of potatoes with them and held as many as I could over the fire.

A few minutes later they were cooked enough to eat, covered with smoke and burned in places but delicious to someone as hungry as I. I finished the first potato, peeled and sliced a second and finished that too. By that time the fire was just a hot bed of graying coals.

There was no water here, but I could see the trees in the distance to my right that marked the bed of a watercourse.

I'd get a drink sometime today. I looked back in the direction I had come for Rafe and Standing Bear, but I didn't see anything.

I began to walk. My feet and legs were stiff and very sore from doing so much walking. I wasn't used to it. Furthermore, riding boots aren't made for walking. The high heels of mine were badly worn on one side and the soles were worn clear through. I was walking on the bacon-rind insoles I'd put in earlier.

A dozen times every hour I looked behind to make sure Rafe and Standing Bear weren't overtaking me. And I watched the land ahead and to my right. What I expected to see, I don't know, but I figured the Indians I'd been with were mad enough over the slaughter of the buffalo they'd been trailing to attack the hunters who had killed them, provided their camp was not too strong.

Along toward midmorning, I saw smoke in the trees that marked the course of the stream on my right. The buffalo hunters' camp, I guessed. Immediately I sought out low ground to travel in, draws and gullies and even, occasionally, a dry wash when there wasn't anything else available. Rafe and Standing Bear might already have reached the buffalo hunters' camp. And even if they had not, my chance of stealing one of the hunters' horses was better if they didn't know I was around.

I had been nearly a mile from the stream. Traveling slowly and carefully, it took me almost an hour to get close enough to see what was going on.

It was immediately apparent to me that there had been a fight. Probably at dawn today. Three bodies lay crumpled on the ground, recognizable as Indians. A dead hunter was lying in the bed of one of the wagons and another, shirtless, had a bloody bandage around his chest. He was sitting on a rock beside the fire, staring glumly into it. Still a third hunter was busy digging a grave for the one who had been killed. None of the others were visible and I guessed they had gone in pursuit of the Indians.

The breeze blew toward me from the camp, bringing the sickening smell of death and rotting flesh. The hides of the buffalo killed yesterday were pegged out on the ground to dry. Other hides, already dry, were stacked six feet high in a dozen piles.

Over close to the nearly dry, sandy bed of the stream there was a corral formed by a single rope stretched between four trees. Inside this corral were five horses. I recognized three of them as having belonged to the Indians. The other two were bigger, stockier.

I stared at the scene, trying to figure out a way to get close enough to the rope corral to steal a horse before the hunter digging the grave or the one at the fire could stop me. Occasionally I glanced back toward the north to be sure Rafe and Standing Bear hadn't yet come into view.

Having decided on the best route, I got up and, crouching low, started toward the streambed and the rope corral. I hadn't gone more than a hundred feet before I heard the sound of horses' hoofs. Glancing up, I saw the remaining four Indians galloping into the hunters' camp.

The one digging the grave scrambled out of it in such haste that he fell before he could reach his gun, leaning against a cottonwood nearby. One of the Indians shot him with an arrow as he got up. The arrow went into his chest. He stood there a moment, both hands on the arrow shaft, trying to pull it out. Then he sat down, already dying but trying to get the arrow out before he died.

The man at the fire had also gotten up. He headed for his own rifle but it was leaning against the wagon wheel, nearly fifty feet away. One of the Indians galloped past him, leaning low to one side, and brained him with an iron tomahawk that buried itself in his skull so deep the handle was yanked out of the Indian's hand. The hunter crumpled and the Indian hauled his plunging horse to a halt. He turned and came back, then dismounted and retrieved his tomahawk.

Now the Indians went to the rope corral and caught their three horses. They led them to the bodies of their comrades and loaded the bodies onto them. They all had braided horsehair ropes and they used these to tie the bodies down. Finally, without a backward look, they rode away, making their horses trot.

It all had happened so fast that I just stood there staring. Only when the Indians had headed away from the camp did I realize that nothing now stood between me and a horse. Furthermore, there were at least two rifles down there and plenty of ammunition for them too.

Best of all, the hunters, when they returned, would assume the Indians had taken the horse and gun. It might puzzle them that both horses and both guns had not been taken, but that circumstance wouldn't change their belief that the Indians were the thieves.

Obviously the four Indians, pursued by the buffalo hunters, had circled back. Which meant the hunters would also be returning soon.

With one last hasty glance toward the north to make sure Rafe and Standing Bear weren't coming, I broke into a run. I reached the hunters' camp and headed immediately for the corral. I got a bridle off the branch of a tree where someone had hung it and then caught the best-looking of the two horses in the corral. I left the rope down so that the other horse could leave if he wanted to. Hurrying, I went to the body of the man who had been digging the grave. His rifle was a big-bore, .52-caliber Spencer repeater. He had a belt of cartridges around his waist. I had to force myself to do it, but I knelt, unbuckled it, and took it off. I buckled it around my own waist, using the last notch in the belt. Even so, it sagged down around my hips.

I jumped up onto the horse. From his back I looked south for the hunters and north once more to make sure neither Rafe nor Standing Bear was yet in sight. Then I drummed on the horse's sides with my heels until he broke into a lumbering trot. I followed the Indians' trail. The hunters would probably not pursue the Indians again, but it wouldn't hurt if they thought the Indians were the ones who had taken their horse.

I stayed with the Indians' trail for about three miles. Then, at a place where brush was thick and grass was high, I turned my horse south, looking back to see how noticeable were the tracks he had made.

I decided they might easily be overlooked, particularly if those pursuing the Indians were hurrying. Feeling better than I had for days about my chances to survive, I headed straight south again toward the Colorado line.

I was sorry for the Indians, but I couldn't muster much sympathy for the buffalo hunters, who were wantonly killing off the animals that meant life to the Indians. I didn't feel bad about stealing either the horse or the rifle. And for the first time, I dared to hope that, in the jumble of tracks in the buffalo hunters' camp, Standing Bear might lose my trail.

Two potatoes weren't really enough to have satisfied my hunger, so I kept my eyes open for antelope or for buffalo and I watched the ground for tracks. All I saw were a few jackrabbits. I didn't bother to try shooting them because I knew if I hit one of them there'd be nothing left but a little bloody fur. At noon, all I could think about was how hungry I was, so when I reached a dry, narrow streambed where there were a few scrub trees for firewood I stopped and built a small fire for myself. While it was getting a start, I went down into the sandy streambed and dug down in the sand with my hands. A foot down I hit water. I kept digging until I had a muddy pool six inches deep. Then I returned to the fire, peeled and sliced three potatoes and cooked them on sticks over the fire. By the time I had finished, the mud and silt had settled in my water hole and I was able to stick my head down into it and drink all I could hold.

Feeling much better, I mounted and headed south again. I rode steadily all afternoon. I suppose it must have been about five o'clock when I heard the faint, distant popping of gunfire.

I stopped and listened, trying to place the exact location of the sounds. They came from straight ahead, or maybe a little to my left. Half a mile away on that heading I could see the scrub trees of the same watercourse where I'd nooned. After I'd crossed it, it had turned south.

I sat there for quite a while, trying to decide what I ought to do. The smart thing would be to keep on going and keep my nose out of places where it didn't belong. For all I knew, the shooting was coming from Rafe and Standing Bear, who might also have run into a bunch of Indians.

Determinedly, I continued riding straight ahead, while the gunfire continued on my left. I had ridden less than a mile when I came to a road.

It wasn't much of a road, only two rutted wheel tracks crossing the prairie grass. But it told me something about what was happening over there where all the gunfire was coming from. Travelers, maybe a wagon, maybe a stagecoach, maybe a horseman or two had been attacked by Indians, probably the same four I'd watched ride away from the buffalo hunters' camp. Their anger over the slaughter of their buffalo still wasn't satisfied, I supposed, and they'd attacked the first whites they'd happened on.

In spite of what had happened with the rustlers, I was scared at the thought of getting into a shooting scrape. But not as much so any more. And I knew it would be on my conscience a long time if I just rode away and ignored the trouble somebody was in over there.

Reluctantly I turned my horse and kicked him into a trot. The shooting was still going on, but the shots were now more widely spaced, as if both sides were conserving what ammunition they had left.

Listening carefully to the reports, I was more convinced than ever that the four Indians had attacked someone traveling on the road. The shots from the Indians' guns, old trapdoor Springfields, were booming, while those from whoever they were attacking were sharper, as if they came from newer guns. Some were flat, as if they were revolver shots.

From about an eighth of a mile, I could better place the exact location of the shots. The Indians were apparently north of the road. I therefore circled to the south, trying to stay behind a low ridge that ran along the south side of the road. Finally, when I was directly abreast of where I figured the beleaguered travelers were, I turned north and cautiously stuck my head above the ridge.

There was a single wagon in the road. One of the horses that had been pulling it was down, dead in the harness. I saw what looked like two women under the wagon. A man had wedged himself between the dead horse and the live one and was returning the Indians' fire from there. I thought that was pretty stupid, because while it might keep him from getting hit, it would practically guarantee that any bullets that missed him had a good chance of hitting the other horse.

I kicked my horse in the ribs, but the best he'd do, even going down the hill, was a jolting trot. Angrily, I beat him on the rump with the barrel of my gun and he finally broke into a grudging lope. Those at the wagon turned their heads to stare at me.

I dismounted, running just before I reached the wagon. First thing I did was tie my horse so that the wagon was between him and the Indians. Then I said to the man, "Mister, you ought to get behind something besides that horse. If you stay there, one of their bullets is sure to hit the other horse."

I guess it was kind of smart aleck for a kid to talk to a grown man like that, but I was beginning to feel less and less like a kid. He looked a little sheepish as he crawled out from behind the dead horse and stood up beside the wagon and looked at me.

He said, "They just started shooting at us. The first shot killed the horse, and after that we couldn't move."

I said, "There's not much daylight left. Soon's it's dark, they'll give it up."

"Who are you?" he asked. "And what are you doing out here all alone?"

I said, "I'm Frank Halliday." I didn't bother with the second part of his question.

He said, "I'm Sam Kroeger. That's Mrs. Overman and her daughter Susan under the wagon."

I peered at the two under the wagon. They were half scared to death. I said, "Ma'am, you and your daughter will be safer in the wagon than under it. They can't see you there." As I spoke, one of the Indians' bullets struck the ground in front of the two and showered them with dirt. They got up and scrambled into the wagon faster than I'd have thought possible.

I crawled under the wagon where they'd been. Kroeger crawled under beside me. I waited until one of the Indians fired, and then I fired the Spencer at the puff of smoke. It kicked like a mule and had a deep-throated roar. I saw the bullet kick up dirt just in front of the clump of brush behind which the Indian was hiding. I said, "They're a long ways off for shooting accurate. Their bullets are mostly going to be short, like mine just was. I thought I'd mention it in case you're worried about the ladies being in the wagon."

He didn't say anything. I looked at him. He was a stocky, muscular man. His hands were calloused and scarred from heavy work. His face had a ruddy quality that labeled him as a man who spent his life outdoors. I'd have said he was a farmer. One thing was sure. He wasn't used to firearms and he wasn't used to somebody shooting at him.

I asked, "What are you doing traveling all alone?"

"We were with a wagon train. Our wagon broke down and they wouldn't wait for us. Took me half a day to get it fixed."

The sun was going down. The Indians fired several more rounds at us, none of which came close. Then I saw them retiring, retreating on foot back to where their horses were.

There was no need for the wagon to be traveling at night. The Indians weren't going to come back tomorrow.

But I'd gotten the idea that if I went with this wagon, maybe I'd shake Rafe and Standing Bear. I said, "Let's get that dead horse out of the harness and put mine in his place. By morning we can be a dozen miles from here."

He looked at me gratefully. "We'd be mighty obliged for the use of your horse, youngster. And for your company."

We got to work unharnessing the dead horse. Having done that, we backed the wagon, using the remaining horse to do it with. Then we harnessed my horse and hitched him beside the other one.

Kroeger climbed to the wagon seat and I climbed up beside him. I put my rifle between my knees, the butt plate on the floorboards. By now it was completely dark, but the horses were able to see the road all right. It seemed strange that a woman and her daughter and an unrelated man would be traveling across country with a wagon train. But then it probably seemed strange to Kroeger that a fifteen-year-old boy would be riding alone across Indian country without even a saddle on his horse.

Maybe I'd tell him and maybe I would not. It was possible Rafe would have posted a reward for my return, calling me a runaway. And these people looked like they could use any money they could put their hands on.

Chapter IX

The only time I was really able to feel safe was at night, because I knew Rafe and Standing Bear couldn't trail me at night. With Kroeger, and both awake and armed, I didn't figure anything was going to happen. A couple of times I thought I'd be making better time if I'd stayed alone, but I had thrown in my lot with these people and I owed it to them to stay with them. At least until they joined up with the main wagon train or reached a good-sized settlement. I knew they couldn't move without my horse.

I didn't worry about the Indians. They had been angry over their losses to the buffalo hunters and had simply been venting their fury when they attacked the wagon. But they wouldn't follow it. I was willing to bet they were on their way back to their village now, taking their dead comrades along with them.

All night we plodded along the two-track, rutted road. The wagon jolted over bumps and swayed from side to side in the crooked ruts. I didn't see how the two women could sleep, but maybe they were used to it.

Kroeger's curiosity finally got the best of him. He asked, "What's a kid your age doing out here in Indian country all alone? You a runaway?"

I didn't answer immediately. He probably thought it was

because I feared he might turn me in, because he said, "Makes no difference to me, son. I ran away myself when I was fourteen, and I figure you're older than that. But I noticed the way you favored your shoulder and there's blood on your shirt. You been shot?"

I realized suddenly that I wanted to tell somebody all that had happened to me. I wanted to get it out of my system. I said, "I'm not exactly a runaway. My pa died several weeks ago. He owned the Halliday Ranch up in Wyoming Territory. He left it to me, but he left it in trust until I would be twenty-one. The trustee was his foreman, Rafe Joslin. Trouble was, Pa put a clause in his will that said if anything happened to me before I reached twenty-one, then the whole shebang would go to Rafe."

Kroeger sounded shocked, "You don't mean that *he* shot you?"

"No. But he made a deal with a couple of rustlers to ambush me. They gave me the shoulder wound."

"How did you get away from them?"

"I didn't. I killed them."

"Good God!" His voice was even more shocked than it had been before. "You've had to grow up fast."

I hadn't thought about it that way before, but I supposed he was right. I had grown up a lot since leaving home. I hadn't changed much physically, because I'd been either hungry or thirsty or both most of the time and I'd sustained a painful if not serious wound. But in terms of self-reliance I wasn't a kid any more. I was a man. I'd come to grips with the world on adult terms and I had survived.

Before I got to feeling too smug about it, I realized that I'd also had a lot of luck. If I hadn't, I'd have been dead a long time ago.

Kroeger asked, "Is the foreman following you now?"

"Uh huh. He and Jack Standing Bear, who breaks horses

for the ranch. Standing Bear is a Sioux and the best tracker on the place."

"Does the Indian know this foreman means to kill you when he catches you?"

"I don't think so. I don't think Standing Bear would stand for it, but he probably won't have much to say. If he objects, Rafe will kill him too."

"Are you absolutely sure this Rafe intends to kill you?"

"I'm sure. I talked to one of the rustlers before he died. He admitted he'd been paid to ambush me."

"My God! I've never heard of such a thing. You're going to have to go to the law. You'll have to tell them this man is trying to kill you."

"I doubt if they'd believe me. Rafe would tell them I'm a runaway. He'd claim the things I say are a pack of lies, the inventions of a kid to try and get out of going home. He might even claim to be my father and I couldn't prove he wasn't."

"What about Standing Bear? Would he just stand there and let Rafe tell those lies?"

"If I know Rafe, Standing Bear won't even be there while he's talking to the sheriff or whoever has me in custody."

"How do you know they'd put you in custody?"

I shrugged. I didn't know. But if I was a lawman and a fifteen-year-old kid came in with a story like mine, I'd probably hold him until his folks showed up. I said, "I guess I'd just rather stay away from the law as long as I can."

Kroeger slapped the backs of the horses with the reins. He was silent awhile and finally he said, "That horse of yours isn't a saddle horse. How'd you come by him?"

I was beginning to think I'd already talked too much and I didn't know whether I could trust Kroeger or not. I didn't know anything about the man, and experience had taught me over the last few weeks that I didn't dare trust anyone.

I didn't want to lie, because I'd never lied. But I didn't see how I could refuse to answer his question without making him even more suspicious than he already was. I said, "I got him from some buffalo hunters. They were attacked by that same bunch of Indians." I left it at that. I had given Kroeger the impression that I'd helped the buffalo hunters against the Indians and that the horse had either been my reward or that I'd bought him from them. I guess the deception succeeded, because he didn't pursue the subject of the horse any more. He said, "You must've gotten the gun from the hunters too. It's a Spencer, isn't it?"

"Uh huh. It belonged to one of the hunters the Indians killed."

There was another long silence and finally Kroeger said, "You can catch yourself some sleep if you want to. Then when you wake up, you can drive and I'll get a little sleep."

I said, "All right," and settled myself as comfortably as I could on the seat. But I didn't go to sleep. I only pretended to. I didn't trust Kroeger. I thought it was possible he'd take my gun while I was asleep and then turn me over to the authorities in the first settlement we reached. He'd get a good gun and a horse they desperately needed out of it.

I was tired and it was hard for me to stay awake. I thought what a hell of a thing it was to distrust everyone you meet, even those you've helped. I remained there silent, slumped in the corner of the wagon seat. Every time I'd feel myself slipping into sleep, I'd pinch my thigh so hard it would wake me up. The hours and the miles passed and finally I sat up with a start, as if I'd awakened suddenly. I said, "I'll drive now if you want to get some sleep."

He handed the reins to me. I supposed I had misjudged him. Or maybe he was just biding his time, believing he would have wakened me if he'd tried to get my gun.

He went to sleep almost immediately and shortly afterward began to snore. I heard a stirring behind me in the wagon and the canvas flap was pulled aside. A girl's voice said, "Mr. Halliday?"

It was the first time I'd ever been called "Mister" in my life. I turned my head. Her face was just a white blur in the darkness, but her voice was soft and pleasant. I said, "What?"

"I just wanted to thank you for all you've done for us. I don't know what we'd have done if you hadn't come along."

I felt embarrassed and didn't know what to say. Finally I said, "I'm glad we didn't have to kill any of those Indians. They found me out on the prairie without a gun or horse and they took me along with them."

"What made them so angry at white people, then?"

"There were seven of them. The youngest was about my age. They were hunting buffalo. They found a trail, but when they reached the end of it, the hide hunters had gotten there first. All the buffalo were dead and skinned and the meat beginning to spoil. It made the Indians furious. One of them was going to kill me but the leader stopped him. They went on to the buffalo hunters' camp. They attacked it and three of them were killed. I don't really blame them for being mad, and I suppose attacking you was just a way of satisfying their anger over all that had happened to them."

"They don't own the buffalo, do they?"

"No. But they depend on buffalo to live. They only kill what they need and they use every last scrap for something or other. The white hunters kill everything in sight and only take the hides. I guess the Indians know that sooner or later all the buffalo will be gone and they'll starve."

Susan was on her knees in the wagon bed, with her arms resting on the back of the wagon seat. She was close enough to stir me up and make me think of the experience I'd had with Mary Jane Meier. The two girls weren't the same, but

I was old enough to know what had happened between me and Mary Jane was a part of a man and woman living together. It was what had been between my father and Rose Moran. It was important and exciting and I didn't need to feel ashamed of the kind of feelings I was having toward Susan Overman.

She said, "I've been listening to you and Mr. Kroeger talk."

I didn't answer because I didn't know what to say.

She asked, "How are you going to get away? What are you going to do?"

"I don't know yet. I'll do the best I can, I guess. Maybe they lost me back there when I left the buffalo hunters' camp. Maybe they think I'm still with the Indians."

"What if they haven't lost you?"

I tried to face that possibility in my mind. I didn't know whether I could kill Rafe Joslin or not, even if I got the chance. It would be almost like killing my father. Rafe Joslin had been around since I'd first started remembering. In some ways he'd been closer to me than my father had.

Much of what I knew I'd learned from Rafe. He'd put me up on my first horse. He'd showed me how to use a rope to catch a calf. I'd learned branding from him and half a hundred other things. He'd never shown me any affection, to be sure, but neither had my father.

I said truthfully, "I don't know. I've been thinking about it and I don't think I could kill Rafe Joslin, even to save my own life. And I know I couldn't kill Standing Bear because he isn't trying to kill me. He's just doing his job, tracking me."

"Maybe you could stay with us. I'll ask Mother tomorrow."

She had said she'd ask her mother. She hadn't said she'd ask Sam Kroeger. She had expressed her curiosity about me and I figured it would be all right if I satisfied mine about Kroeger. I asked, "What's Mr. Kroeger to you? An uncle or something?"

"No. He's just a man Mother hired to drive the wagon for us. They wouldn't take us on the wagon train unless we had a man with us."

He was sitting right beside me but he was snoring and I figured he was asleep. I asked, "What do you think of him? Do you like him?"

Her voice dropped to a whisper. "Not really. He keeps making up to Mother, so I don't trust him, I guess. It's just a feeling that I have."

I said, "That's about the way I felt about him. I think he'd turn me over to the law to get my horse and gun."

Susan must have been uneasy about talking about Kroeger with him so close, because she changed the subject suddenly. "Where is your ranch and how big is it?"

"It's up north of here about a hundred and fifty miles. I don't know how big it is and I don't know how many cattle are on it, but I'd guess maybe it's a couple of hundred thousand acres and there are at least fifty thousand head of cattle."

I could tell she was impressed. "No wonder your foreman is willing to kill you to get his hands on it."

I said, "He's more than a foreman, really. My father and mother settled on the ranch in sixty-five, just after the Sand Creek Massacre. I was only a year old at the time. About a year later, Rafe Joslin rode by and stayed for the night. He never left. My first memories are of Rafe Joslin being foreman. I figure my father should have left him part of the ranch, and I told the lawyer I was willing to give him part of it. But the lawyer said I couldn't give anything I didn't own, and I wouldn't own the Halliday Ranch until I was twenty-one."

"Couldn't you have told Mr. Joslin that you meant to give him part of the ranch?"

"Maybe. Only I couldn't figure a way of doing it that wouldn't sound like I was passing out charity to him. The truth is, he's earned a part of the ranch and nobody should have to give him what he's already earned."

She was silent for a while. When she spoke, her voice was very soft. "I think you are a very fine person, Mr. Halliday."

I turned my head and leaned toward her. Her face was just a blur in the darkness, but there was a clean fragrance about her that stirred me up. I kissed her, aiming for her mouth but missing and kissing her on the nose instead. She laughed, then reached out and with both hands brought my head toward her, straight this time. Her lips were soft and warm.

The kiss made me want more. I could feel my heart beating faster and my blood pounding through my veins. I asked, "Where are you heading, in case I have to run?"

"Denver. Mother's going to start some kind of business there. Maybe a dressmaking shop. Maybe a bakery. She hasn't made up her mind for sure."

"What about your father? What happened to him?"

"He was killed in the war. In the last battle before the surrender at Appomattox."

"Then you never knew him, did you?"

"No. I have no memories of him at all."

"And your mother has never remarried?"

"No."

Next to me, Sam Kroeger stirred, sat up straight and yawned. He stretched his arms. He asked sleepily, "Is everything all right?"

I said, "Sure. I've been talking to Miss Overman."

He said, "I'll take it now." I handed him the reins. Susan Overman withdrew from her position and went into the wagon. I wondered if Sam Kroeger had really been asleep or if he had only been feigning it the way I had. I made up my mind I was going to keep an eye on him.

I hadn't definitely promised that I would look her up if and when I got away from Rafe, but I'd pretty well let her know I would. I'd asked where she would be, in case I got away from Rafe, and that was about the same as telling her I didn't want to let her go out of my life.

I wondered exactly how old she was. Old enough, I guessed. Out here, people got married lots of times when the man was sixteen or seventeen, the girl not more than fifteen.

I'd been doing a man's work for several years. I'd made some mistakes while I'd been fleeing from Rafe and Standing Bear, but they were mistakes any grown man might have made. The point was, I was alive. I had coped with being hunted, and so far I had survived. I figured if I survived until Rafe was either dead or in jail for trying to murder me, I'd be man enough not only to take over the Halliday Ranch but to take a wife as well. And from what I'd seen of her, Susan Overman was going to make somebody a damn good wife. She was used to the hardship of traveling across country in a wagon, against which the hardship of living on a ranch like Halliday would seem like pure luxury.

There was room for her mother there. There was even room for Kroeger, if he turned out to be trustworthy. But I doubted if he would.

Chapter X

At dawn we stopped in a grove of trees at the side of a wide, dry streambed. While the two women gathered wood for a fire, Kroeger and I unharnessed the horses and led them to the sandy streambed. We dug down in the sand with our hands and when we had a pool of water, let the horses drink. I took them then and led them to where there was some grass. I staked them out with a couple of ropes that had been in the wagon so that they could graze. I checked my horse over to make sure the collar hadn't chafed. I was relieved to discover that it had not.

By now I could smell bacon cooking, and sourdough biscuits, and I realized how damn hungry I really was. I helped Kroeger to fill the water casks on the side of the wagon with water from the hole we'd dug. The sediment had settled and the water was nearly clear.

Susan kept throwing glances at me and I kept throwing glances at her and every now and then our eyes would meet. Usually she'd flush when they did, and I took this to be a good sign. If she didn't give a damn about me it wouldn't embarrass her to look at me. I caught myself thinking about my experience with Mary Jane Meier and wondering if it would be the same with Susan. Better, I thought. Mary Jane Meier had been a chippie for all her tender years. She'd led me along in everything that had happened. I didn't think Susan would be like that. We'd be exploring it together, with me leading the way, and that was how it ought to be. Besides, I realized that I felt a tenderness toward Susan I hadn't felt toward Mary Jane. I remembered the way she'd taken my face between her hands and steered me to a kiss that didn't miss its mark.

We ate breakfast. They had some sorghum molasses for the sourdough biscuits that I found delicious, having had nothing sweet since leaving home. Afterward, the two women cleaned the plates and the skillet while Kroeger and I led the horses to the wagon, backed them into place and hitched them up.

We were on the road not long after the sun came up. The horses were tired from having traveled all night, but they'd been watered and had had a chance to graze awhile. Kroeger kept them at a plodding walk.

He and Mrs. Overman wanted to catch up with the wagon train if possible. When they did, they'd be able to borrow a horse and I'd be free to leave. I didn't know whether I would or not. For one thing, I was tired of being hunted game. For another, I didn't want to leave Susan Overman. I knew how scarce young, pretty, unmarried women were in Denver and in the mining country west of it. I knew there was a good chance she'd find somebody else before I could manage to get to Denver and locate her. It was too soon, of course, but I wanted to talk to her and try to tell her how I felt and ask her to wait. At least for a little while.

Several miles from where we'd stopped for breakfast, Susan suddenly dropped from the rear of the wagon and began to walk, on the windward side of the wagon out of the dust. Kroeger was driving, so there was nothing to keep me on the seat. I jumped down and joined Susan.

She said, "It's a beautiful morning."

I hadn't noticed but it was. The sky was a flawless blue. The sun was warm without being hot. The meadowlarks trilled, their songs almost continuous. A hawk soared high above us.

Apparently neither of us was very good at small talk. Finally, after the silence had become awkward, I said, "I'm not going to be running from Rafe forever. And I'll be sixteen in a couple of days. How old are you?"

"Fifteen. I'll be sixteen in September."

I was blunt. I said, "That's not too young."

"For what?"

"For getting hitched. I never met a girl like you. I wish you'd wait for me until I get clear of Rafe. I'll come to Denver and find you someway."

It was one of the things I liked about her. Her straightforwardness. She said simply, "I'll wait."

I said, "Our ranch house is huge. There'll be all the room in the world for your ma."

She said, "You're proposing to me. And you haven't known me more than a day and night."

I said, "I've known Rafe all my life. I'd never have believed he'd try to kill me for the ranch. I don't reckon time has much to do with deciding what kind of person someone is."

She said, "This isn't the way I'd thought it would be."

"Thought what would be?"

"Being proposed to. And accepting."

I said, "Then you are accepting?"

"Yes."

I wanted to stop and hold her. I wanted to kiss her, but there was her mother and Kroeger, probably watching everything we did. I said, "What's it supposed to be like?"

She smiled, her eyes warm as they met mine. "I don't know. Moonlight. The smell of flowers. Maybe a swing."

I said, "Nothing like that out here. But I'll tell you one thing. I'll be good to you. You'll never be sorry."

She linked her arm with mine and squeezed. Right then the wagon descended into a dry wash and for a moment we couldn't see it, and neither Kroeger nor Susan's mother could see us. A little awkwardly I turned toward her and put my arms around her. I lowered my head and kissed her on the mouth.

I was stirred like I'd never been before. I guess she was too, because she looked flustered as she drew away. She said softly, "Be careful, Frank. Don't let Rafe Joslin get to you."

"He won't. I've stayed away from him so far and I'm not going to let him get me now." I was thinking that now I could kill Rafe if it was in defense of my life. I supposed I'd always enjoyed life, but it had been composed of a lot more work than play.

Now there was more. More than I'd ever dreamed there'd be. There was Susan, and the promise of a life with her. Maybe it meant more to me than it would have had my father given me the normal affection a father gives his son. Maybe it meant more because I'd never known my mother, and so had never known what it was to be loved.

Maybe the reason Susan and I had been drawn to each other so quickly and so powerfully was for that reason. Susan had never known her father's love, since he'd been killed in the war long before she was able to remember him. My mother had died before I was able to remember her.

The wagon climbed out of the dry wash and Susan and I released each other and resumed our walk. But now there was something definite between us, something pledged.

I walked with Susan until both of us were tired. Then I

boosted her up over the wagon tailgate and hurried around and climbed to the seat myself.

We made no stop for nooning, since everybody was anxious to catch the wagon train if possible. Kroeger thought it likely that we'd catch them shortly after dark tonight because of the fact that we'd traveled all the night before.

He was right. It was about an hour after sundown when we spotted the wagon train camped ahead of us. More than a dozen fires winked in the darkness. As we drew closer I could see the grouped, canvas-topped wagons. They had not found either water or timber and had camped on the open plain.

We drove in, and people clustered around the wagon, greeting Mrs. Overman and Susan, calling out to Kroeger with what seemed to be less cordiality. He halted the wagon at the edge of the camp and I helped him unhitch the horses and turn them in with the others, being herded by two boys about my age.

There was some kindling wood in the wagon and a plentiful supply of buffalo chips if you got a hundred yards or so from the wagons. Kroeger and I both gathered them and built a fire. Grace Overman and Susan prepared supper, which tonight consisted of rice with gravy made in the pan in which the bacon had been cooked this morning. There was something they called coffee, not real coffee but a drink made from roasted beans. It was hot, though, and I drank it eagerly.

We were just finishing when I saw the two riders come into camp. They were fifty yards away, but when they passed the first campfire I recognized them instantly. It was Rafe, and Standing Bear was riding immediately behind. I supposed I should have known that nothing was going to throw Standing Bear off the trail.

My gun was leaning against one of the wagon wheels.

There was no time now to catch my horse. They'd have me before I even cut him out of the bunch. I grabbed my gun and started away, remembering Susan as I did. She was still beside the fire. I didn't dare let any light fall on me if I could help it, so from the darkness I called, "Susan!"

She turned.

I said, "That's them. I've got to go." I didn't wait to hear what she said, if anything. I was already moving away deeper into the darkness.

I knew I couldn't steal a horse from these travelers. But there was nothing to prevent me from taking either Rafe's or that of Standing Bear. They were going to leave their horses and walk to one of the fires so that they could question the travelers.

I circled the camp, staying out far enough so that none of the people could see me. It wasn't hard. All eyes were on the two strangers who had ridden into camp. They were as different as night from day from the people in the wagon train, who were mostly farmers and shopkeepers. Rafe and Standing Bear were cowmen and they looked like it.

I made a complete half circle of the camp. Rafe and Standing Bear were at one of the fires talking to a couple of men. Their horses stood ground-tied fifty yards away, right at the edge of the fire's light.

I thought, "Why take only one horse? If I take both, they won't be able to follow me until they get some more."

Walking as silently and as carefully as I could, doing it the way a buffalo hunter approaches a herd of buffalo, straight on with no sideways movement to catch their eyes, I moved toward the horses of Rafe and Standing Bear. Now I was fifty feet away. Now thirty. Now ten.

Suddenly, for no reason I could understand, Rafe turned and looked straight at me. Maybe it was the intensity with which I had been looking at him which drew his glance. I didn't know.

He let out a yell. He started toward me.

No time now for stealing Rafe's horse too. Standing Bear's was closest. The right-hand rein was looped around the saddle horn. The left was trailing on the ground.

I hit the saddle just as Rafe let out a formless yell. I drummed my heels on the horse's sides and at the same time whacked him on the rump with the barrel of the Spencer.

I was laying low over the horse's withers as he surged into a startled run. Behind me, Rafe's rifle barked, and barked again. Both shots missed.

Apparently stung by his failure to get me with his first two shots, he took more time with the third. This one grazed the horse's rump and for a moment I thought he was going to stop running and start to buck. But I kept his head up and he changed his mind about wanting to buck and only ran faster than he had before.

With the horse running, there was nothing more that I could do. I glanced behind and saw Rafe, kneeling now, taking a careful bead on my rapidly disappearing form.

He fired, but just as he did, Standing Bear kicked the rifle barrel and it discharged pointing nearly forty-five degrees away from me. Rafe got up, jacked another cartridge in and jammed the rifle into the belly of Standing Bear.

I thought he was going to shoot, but I heard no report and Standing Bear did not fall. Rafe must have changed his mind, controlled his fury and disappointment, because he lowered the rifle and strode swiftly after his horse.

Then I went over a slight rise and the camp, Rafe, and Standing Bear were lost to view.

I could hardly control the elation that I felt. I had a good horse under me once more. I might have taken him, but I hadn't stolen him. He really belonged to me because he had an H Quarter Circle brand on his hip.

Furthermore, they couldn't follow me at night. Nor could they follow me tomorrow unless they could talk one of the travelers into selling them a horse. Even then the horse they got would probably be too heavy and too slow.

Once more I had a lead of six or eight hours at the very least. I was no worse off than when I had left home.

I thought of Susan Overman. I didn't want to risk losing her. She was going to Denver. As far as I was concerned, that meant I had to go to Denver too.

Somehow, someway, I might be able to get help from the law in a town the size of Denver. And even if I couldn't, it was big enough maybe for me to hide from Rafe.

Having made the decision as to which way I wanted to go, I circled west of the wagon camp until I located the road. I put my recently acquired horse into it. At a steady trot, I headed west.

Standing Bear's horse was tired, so every hour I halted him, took the saddle off and cooled his back. But tired or not, he'd have to keep going all tonight and all day tomorrow. I didn't know how far Denver was, but it couldn't be much more than a couple of days' ride. I'd know when daylight came tomorrow, I thought. I'd know how close it was when I saw the Rockies looming on the horizon ahead of me.

Chapter XI

When dawn came I stopped, unsaddled, and fanned the horse's back to cool it off. Then I staked him out with Standing Bear's lariat and a stake I found in his saddlebags. Besides the stake I found quite a bit of jerky. I got a couple of pieces of it and, occasionally drinking from his canteen, watched the horse graze, watched the road behind me, and watched the sun come up.

When I had finished the jerky, I got the saddlebags off Standing Bear's horse and went through them. I found a razor, shaving soap and brush, a comb, and some extra cartridges for the Spencer rifle he'd yanked from the saddle boot when he got off the horse last night. I also found a couple of dirty shirts and a buckskin bag that felt like it was full of lead. I looked in. There were ten fifty-dollar gold pieces in it.

For several moments I stood there staring at one I held in my hand. It was new and shiny and had probably just come from a bank somewhere. To me, there was only one possible explanation for its presence in Standing Bear's saddlebag. It was a payoff from Rafe. For tracking me. For helping him run me to earth. Maybe it was the price of my death, but when the chips were down, Standing Bear hadn't been able to let Rafe murder me. He'd knocked the gun aside.

There was something else in the saddlebag. A dog-eared, nearly worn-out calendar. All the earlier sheets had been thrown away right up to the one for July. On it each date had been crossed out as it had passed. The first one that hadn't was July twenty-ninth, and that was my birthday. I was sixteen years old today.

I returned the things to the saddlebags, keeping out one of the gold pieces and putting it into my pocket. I'd buy some supplies first chance I got. I figured the gold was probably mine anyway. If it wasn't, I could return it to Standing Bear when I got safely home again. If I ever did.

One thing I decided then and there. Five hundred dollars was probably more money than Standing Bear had ever had at one time or was ever likely to. The horse I'd taken from him might belong to the Halliday Ranch, but the saddle was his own. He'd stay with Rafe. He'd continue helping him run me to earth. Next time, having gotten used to the idea, he probably wouldn't interfere when Rafe tried killing me.

The horse had been grazing more than an hour and seemed rested. I saddled him, mounted and rode out again, staying on the narrow road and keeping the horse at a steady trot.

I wondered what my father would think if he could see me now. He'd probably approve of me. I had two very capable men after me, trying to kill me, and so far I'd managed to keep them from doing it. Moreover, my father would probably regret the arbitrary age he'd put into his will as the age I'd have to reach before I'd be a man. I'd either be a man a lot sooner, right away in fact, or I'd end up dead before I ever got to be twenty-one or even seventeen.

I stared westward, looking for the peaks of the Continental Divide, but the morning haze kept me from seeing them. Finally, near noon, I saw the jagged line that marked the Divide, dim with distance, but unmistakable.

Shortly after first glimpsing the Rockies, I brought a two-story log building into view. There was a big corral out behind the place in which there were eight horses, not saddle horses but the heavier kind used for pulling wagons or stagecoaches. There was an old mud wagon beside the corral, one used probably for short runs. Besides the eight coach horses in the corral there were two saddle horses. And, tied to the hitch rail in front of the stage stop, there were three other horses with saddles on them.

I reached the place and swung stiffly to the ground. I tied my horse beside the three and went inside.

The room was huge, with leather-covered sofas and chairs, Indian or Mexican rugs on the floor, a fireplace at one side. One end of the room was occupied by two tables that must have been at least twenty feet long, with benches on either side. Just beyond this dining area there was a closed-off kitchen, from which issued some of the most appetizing smells I had encountered in a long, long time. A stairway led to the upstairs where there were probably bedrooms for guests.

All the occupants of the room looked curiously at me as I came in. There were three young bearded men, probably the owners of the three horses tied outside. There were two other men, one bearded and middle-aged, the other with a couple or three days' growth of whiskers on his face. There was an ample Anglo woman with gray hair and two younger Mexican women, probably kitchen helpers. The middle-aged, bearded man called out heartily, "Howdy, son. We're all getting ready to sit down to dinner. You can wash out back."

I had the Spencer in my hand. I didn't put it down. I crossed the room and went out the back door, briefly worried about the gold in the saddlebags on my horse. I put the worry aside. Nobody would expect it to be there and therefore would probably not risk tampering with someone else's saddlebags.

There was a pump behind the building, a couple of wash-pans and a piece of homemade soap. I washed and dried on the dirty towel that was hanging on the pump. Then, picking up my rifle, I went back inside. I took a place at the table, still keeping the rifle beside me, being the only one at the table who did. The three men who owned the horses outside all had revolvers and they kept them strapped around their waists, so I wasn't the only one at the table who was armed.

The women carried in the food. I'd been eating pretty slim for a long time and I ate like this meal was going to be my last. The three bearded young men kept looking at me and finally one of them said, "You all alone, kid?"

I nodded, my mouth full of food.

"Where you headed?"

"West."

"Runaway?"

I finished chewing the food I had in my mouth, took a gulp of coffee and looked at him. I was getting tired of being called "kid" and being treated like a kid. Most of all I was getting tired of being preyed on by men who thought I was a runaway. I said, "Mister, I'm not asking you your business, and I'll thank you not to ask me mine."

The middle-aged man, who apparently ran the stage station, laughed. The man who had asked me if I was a runaway flushed with anger and his eyes glittered. I knew I should have simply denied being a runaway and let it go at that, but I hadn't. It probably wouldn't have made any difference anyway. If the three were honest they wouldn't bother me even if I had angered them. If they weren't, it wouldn't make any difference whether I angered them or not. They'd still try to rob me.

I finished eating and drained what was left in my coffee cup. I got up from the table. The three men left money on the table for their meal, but all I had was the fifty-dollar gold piece and I didn't want them to see it if it could be helped. I went across the big room to a counter behind which there were cubbyholes with room keys like in a hotel, and waited there for the man who ran the place. In a glass case beneath the counter there were a number of items with price tags on them, things I supposed travelers who had run out of money had sold to the man who ran the place. Among these items was a revolver, a Navy Colt .36-caliber percussion piece that had been converted to hold thirty-eight cartridges. There was a belt and holster with it and the belt was filled with cartridges. When the man came over, I asked to look at it. The price on it was sixteen dollars.

More than the gun I wanted to give the man some incentive for changing my fifty-dollar gold piece. He'd balk at changing it for a twenty-five-cent meal and would probably kick up a fuss. If I bought the gun, maybe he'd make change willingly.

I looked it over, tried the action to make sure it worked, then said, "I'll take it," and laid the fifty-dollar gold piece on the counter. He looked at me suspiciously. "You steal this money, kid?"

I looked straight back at him. "No, sir." Maybe in a way I had stolen the money, but it had come, I was sure, out of the five thousand my father had left to Rafe. I figured he had paid it to Standing Bear for helping him track me down and kill me, and I figured both of them had forfeited any right to it. Anyhow, if I survived and inherited the Halliday Ranch, I could repay it, and that changed the ethics of how I had come by the money some.

I don't think the man believed me but he had no real grounds for disbelieving, and besides he wanted to sell the gun. He took the fifty and disappeared into a small office behind the counter. When he came back he counted out my change—a twenty-dollar gold piece, a ten, and some silver dollars and smaller change. I noticed the three bearded men watching all this carefully, though all of them looked away when I turned around and looked straight at them. I'd been foolish for letting it be known I had money, but I'd had to eat. I asked the man, "Will you have a sack of grub fixed up for me?"

"Sure." He headed toward the kitchen. I strapped on the Navy Colt, feeling self-conscious as I did. It sagged pretty low because I was so skinny, but I guessed it would stay up. Pretty soon the man came back with a gunnysack. He said, "A dollar will do it, I guess."

I gave him a dollar and took the sack. Then, with my rifle in one hand, the sack in the other, I went outside. I tied on the sack, shoved the rifle down into the saddle boot and untied my horse. I mounted and headed west again.

The eastern Colorado plains aren't flat. They're rolling, a lot like they are up home, and sometimes you see a bluff with a gray sandstone rim. I kept my eyes straight ahead until I came to the first drop in the road. Then I turned and looked behind.

I could still see the stage station. I could also see the three men about halfway between me and the stage depot.

I was beginning to feel more and more like hunted game. Every time I got a horse and a gun it seemed like there was somebody who wanted to rob me of them. The only ones that hadn't tried to take anything from me were the Indians and the folks on the wagon train. The Indians had helped me even though they knew I hadn't anything to give them in return.

For a while I debated what I ought to do. I could turn either north or south. Then, if the three followed me, I'd know, at least, what their intentions were.

Nothing was going to make much difference so far as Rafe and Standing Bear were concerned. They'd trail me no matter where I went. Then I had a new idea. Maybe when the stage came along, I could flag it down and buy passage to Denver on it. I could tie my horse behind. I shook my head. He would still leave tracks and Standing Bear would follow them.

Or I could turn the horse loose and let the three men who were following take possession of him. The stage would go on, with me inside, and the three would fall behind. When Rafe and Standing Bear caught up with them, it was almost certain that they'd try to recover Standing Bear's horse. Going up against three men, there was a good chance one or both of them would either be wounded or killed.

It would have been a good idea except for one thing. I'd let the three men following me know that I had some gold. They didn't know how much, but even if it was only the change for the fifty, they weren't going to be satisfied with my horse. They'd want the gold as well.

Still, it seemed the only chance I had. It was barely possible the three men would be satisfied with the horse. And with nearly five hundred dollars in gold, I'd have no trouble getting another one.

My mind was made up. Occasionally I glanced behind. The three kept the same distance between themselves and me. They were waiting for the right place, or the right time, I supposed, before closing in. I hoped the stage came along before they decided the time was right. I'd gone up against unfavorable odds before and come out all right, but that didn't mean I always would. I'd been lucky so far, but I couldn't count on continued luck.

About midmorning I passed a stage heading east. Both driver and shotgun guard raised a hand in greeting. I couldn't see whether there were any passengers inside or not, but the presence of the shotgun guard indicated that the stage must be carrying gold. Probably from the mines in the mountains west of Denver.

The westbound stage ought to be coming soon. I kept looking back for it, but it was almost noon before I saw it and the dust cloud it raised from the road.

Leaving my horse behind was sure to raise questions in the minds of the stage driver and guard. I tried to think of a logical explanation, finally settling on telling them I had ridden to the road to catch the stage from the ranch where I lived, a dozen miles to the south. The horse, I would say, would return home if I tied up the reins. I would say my grandfather had died in Denver and that I was going to the funeral. It wasn't the most logical explanation in the world, I guessed, but it was all that I could come up with suddenly.

I waved as the stage approached. It pulled to a stop and the dust cloud it raised rolled foward and enveloped me. To the driver I yelled, "I want passage to Denver!"

"What you going to do with that horse?"

"Tie up his reins and turn him loose. I live about ten miles south of here. He'll go home."

He yelled, "From here to Denver will be six dollars!"

"All right."

"What you going to Denver for? You a runaway?"

I was sure getting tired of that question, but getting mad now wasn't going to do me any good. I said, "My grandpa just died in Denver. I'm going to the funeral."

He nodded, apparently accepting that explanation. I dismounted and tied my horse's reins up. I hated to get into the coach, because if Rafe and Standing Bear caught up it would be like a trap. But I was committed now. I opened the door and climbed inside, carrying my rifle and the saddlebags.

There was a woman in the coach and two men. The woman was pretty and young, and dressed fancier than any woman I had ever seen before. One of the men was dressed pretty near as fancy as she was. The other wore work clothes and miners' boots. I stuck my head out the window and looked back as we pulled away. My horse didn't seem to know what to do. He trotted after the coach for a little ways, then stopped and stood there looking after us. The three men came into sight back about a quarter mile. When they saw the horse standing there, they urged their horses into a lope. I saw them catch Standing Bear's horse before we dipped down into another draw.

The man with the fancy clothes asked, "Where you going, son?"

"Denver. My grandpa's funeral." I thought that since leaving home I'd not only become a liar. I'd become a thief. And a killer. I could justify myself, of course. I hadn't lied unless it was necessary. I hadn't stolen except to make it possible for me to survive. And I hadn't killed except in self-defense.

Maybe my father would condemn the things I had done. But I didn't think he would. Nobody can be blamed for trying to stay alive. And nobody should stand unresisting and let somebody murder him.

Chapter XII

Every time we'd come to a high point in the road, I stuck
my head out the window to look back. The three strangers
from the stagecoach way station had caught Standing Bear's
horse, but they hadn't stopped coming and they seemed to
be trying to keep up with the stage.

The coach was traveling pretty fast, the horses mostly at
a lope. Every half hour or so the driver would slow them
down to a walk for about ten or fifteen minutes. Then
they'd be off at a lope again. I supposed the stagecoach way
stations were pretty close together along this road. Otherwise the driver wouldn't have dared use up the horses that
way.

It was about midafternoon when we brought the next
way station into sight. I looked back one final time. I saw
the three pursuers stop their horses and ride out of sight into
a draw. They were following me, intending to rob me of
what gold I had and my two guns. But they didn't want to
do it with half a dozen witnesses looking on. They'd wait,
and try to catch me alone, even if they had to follow all the
way to Denver, which was probably where they were going
anyway.

I wished Rafe and Standing Bear would catch up with
them, but there wasn't very much chance of it. Standing

Bear wouldn't have been able to get another horse as good as the one he'd had.

The coach pulled up at the way station in a cloud of dust. The driver yelled, "Ten-minute stop, folks," and the man who ran the way station opened the coach door and helped the woman alight. Her perfume was strong when she moved and her silk skirts rustled. The man who had spoken to me got out next, and the man in work clothes after that. I got out last, and handed the ten-dollar gold piece to the driver to pay my fare. He gave me four silver dollars change.

Before going into the station, I looked back the way we had come. The three who had Standing Bear's horse were nowhere to be seen. They were going to stay out of sight until the stagecoach left, I thought. When it did, they'd follow it.

There was one way I could avoid them. I could stay here when the stage pulled out. I could hide someplace.

On the way into the station, I caught the driver's arm. "I think I'll stay here and maybe catch the next stage."

He shrugged. "Suit yourself." He handed me a ticket so I could board a later stage without paying the fare again.

I walked straight through the station and out the back door. There were two outhouses. I waited my turn, letting the other two men and the driver and guard go ahead of me. When they had all come out, I went in and closed the door.

There were wide cracks in the walls and I could see the road for a long ways back in the direction we had come. The three horsemen were still not visible. I knew I was gambling—that the horsemen wouldn't stop, or if they did they wouldn't inquire as to whether or not I had been on the stage when it left. If they did and were told I had stayed here, then my chances weren't very good.

Because of the building between the stagecoach and the

outhouse, I couldn't see when the other three passengers boarded the stage. But I did see the coach pull away, the driver cracking his whip over the fresh team's heads, the guard on the seat at his side. It raised a cloud of dust as it pulled away, and then it was gone from my view.

I kept watching the road leading toward the northeast. After several minutes the three horsemen appeared, one leading the horse that had belonged to Standing Bear. They didn't stop at the stage station but rode straight on past, keeping their horses at a lope.

I came out of the outhouse. I was between two fires now. Rafe and Standing Bear were behind me, the three who intended to rob me ahead. I went into the building. "How long before the next stage comes through?" I asked the man who ran the place.

"Late tonight. How come you weren't on that one?"

"Missed it," I lied. "But I got to get to Denver. You got a horse that I can buy?"

"There's two in the corral. A hundred dollars and you take your pick."

I said, "You got a deal, provided you loan me a pair of your boots and keep your mouth shut about it afterward."

"You *are* a runaway."

"Maybe I am. I'm sure as hell not the first. You want to sell one of those nags out there for twice what it's worth or not?"

"All right." He sat down and pulled off his boots. I took mine off and put his on. My feet swam around in them, but I went out, took my pick of the two saddle horses in the corral, put a bridle on him and led him to the front door of the way station. I went inside, gave the man two fifty-dollar gold pieces, and put my own boots back on. I said, "We've got a deal. I expect you to keep your end of it."

"Who's after you?"

I decided it would be a good idea if I let him have the whole story. I said, "All right, I'll tell you all of it. My pa was killed a few weeks ago when a horse fell with him. He owned a big ranch up in Wyoming. He left it to me, but he made the foreman trustee until I'd be twenty-one. The trouble was, he put a clause in the will that if something happened to me before I turned twenty-one, the place would go to the foreman. So the foreman set out to see that I never got to be twenty-one. Soon as I knew what he was up to, I ran away. He's still after me, and he'll be through here, along with an Indian tracker, sometime today." I stopped a minute and then I said, "You give me your name, and if you keep still about selling me a horse, I'll see you get repaid."

He hesitated a moment, and I knew that if he got a better offer from Rafe he'd sell me out without a second thought. He got a piece of paper, though, and wrote his name on it. I put it in my pocket, went out the front door. Careful where I stepped, I vaulted to the back of the horse I'd bought. I'd been riding bareback since I'd been about four years old, so I didn't need a saddle. I headed down the road the way the stage had gone and, a quarter mile away, looked back to see the man standing there watching me. I knew damned good and well he'd spill his guts to Rafe and take whatever Rafe gave him in preference to waiting until I sent something to him later on.

I kept watching for a place where I could leave the road without making tracks and I finally found it. A dry wash crossed the road and the road dipped into it and climbed out again. The bottom of the dry wash was covered with gravel and sandstone rocks that wouldn't show a trail, at least not an identifiable one.

I turned off the road and followed the dry wash for more than half a mile before I climbed the horse out of it. I halted on a high point of ground and stared back in the direction I had come. I couldn't see the stage station or anything on the road that headed east.

The road leading toward Denver was equally empty. I felt a moment's elation. Maybe, at last, I had shaken off the pursuit. Then I remembered the station agent back there at the stage depot and I knew I was dreaming. He was going to give me away, just as sure as hell. Rafe and Standing Bear weren't going to be following the coach. They were going to be looking for a horse's tracks, and it would be easy enough for Standing Bear to pick out the tracks of the horse I was riding because they would overlie those of the stagecoach horses and those of the three men who had followed the stage.

I was right back where I had started from. Maybe, I thought, if I had given the man at the stage depot a hundred dollars, he'd have kept his big mouth shut. Then I shook my head. He wouldn't. He'd have taken my hundred dollars and then, scenting more, would have betrayed me to Rafe and Standing Bear, getting another hundred or so from Rafe.

All right. Rafe and Standing Bear would be coming after me. But I was well armed now. I had a good rifle and plenty of ammunition for it. I had a revolver and a belt filled with cartridges. I had a horse and a sack of grub. I was in better shape than at any time since leaving home.

I tried to put into practice all the things I had learned from Standing Bear over the years. There are lots of ways of hiding a trail. You ride in rocky places. You ride in gulches or ravines when the skies threaten rain. You ride in roads or cattle trails where there is a good chance your tracks will be quickly obliterated by other tracks.

But the best I could hope for would be to slow Standing

Bear. I'd never throw him off. He was too good for me to fool him very long.

There was an ultimate solution but I hadn't accepted it. I had to ambush both Rafe and Standing Bear. I had to kill them both. Only when I had would I be able to return to the Halliday Ranch. Only then would I be safe.

For now, my best chance lay in making good time. I doubted if Standing Bear would have been able to obtain a good horse, one that would keep up with Rafe's high-spirited black. So time was on my side.

I still wanted to go to Denver, so, while I continued away from the road for a couple of miles, I still tried to keep the tree-lined river bottom in sight. It was bounded on the south by a ridge and a lot of rounded hills beyond, so the task wasn't difficult.

Keeping my horse at a trot and looking behind often, I rode southwest. My rifle rested across my knees. I didn't know it, but I'd have been a lot better off if I'd gone the other way and followed the river bottom, even though riding there would have been slower and more difficult. No matter how I tried to stay hidden, I was skylined at regular intervals.

Neither did I know that the three who had followed me from the stage depot had overtaken the stage within five miles after it had left the stage depot. The excuse they had used for stopping it was that I had left my horse and they wanted to return it to me.

A thin excuse maybe, but one that might be accepted no matter how far-fetched it seemed.

But I did see them while they were still half a mile away, and I knew they had seen me and were planning to intercept and ambush me.

Immediately, I started looking around for a place to hide. There was nothing. Right here, the prairie was as flat as I had seen it yet. There was nothing for me to do but flee. I whirled my horse and drummed on his sides with my heels. When he refused to gallop, I flailed his rump with the barrel of my rifle and he finally, reluctantly, broke into a lope.

Glancing behind, I saw the three, still leading Standing Bear's horse, also galloping.

I looked ahead. Three against one were lousy odds, and unless I found some way to even them, I was going to be killed before Rafe and Standing Bear even had another chance at me.

In the distance, about a mile away, there was a bluff, rising to a height of no more than a hundred feet above the surrounding plain. From where I was I couldn't tell if there was any cover or not, but there couldn't be any less than there was right here.

Behind, the three were gaining. My horse wasn't the best I'd ever ridden, not nearly as fast as Standing Bear's horse or as the mounts of the three behind. I kept beating him over the rump with my rifle barrel to keep him at a lope. His neck began to sweat.

I was sweating too, but I wasn't scared any more. I was mad and getting madder all the time. Fear had already been scared out of me, I guess, by other things that had happened to me before.

I was half tempted to stop, and turn, and fight it out right here. But not tempted enough to seriously consider it. I was mad, but I hadn't taken leave of my senses yet. When I took on the three chasing me I wanted something, some kind of cover that would even up the odds.

The bluff grew closer but so did the three men following. It looked like a toss-up whether they'd get in rifle range of me before I reached the bluff or not.

I crested a ridge running parallel to the bluff and could see the base of it for the first time. There was a grove of scrubby trees at the foot of the bluff, maybe where a spring rose, and at the base of the trees the sagebrush was thick. The trouble was, the grove could be surrounded, leaving me no escape. The only good thing about it was that the three I'd be shooting at would be in the open and I'd be hidden in those trees.

I headed for it, since it was the only cover in sight. But as I got closer to it, I saw that the spring that had nurtured the trees and sagebrush actually rose about a hundred feet up on the slope of the bluff. It was choked with brush so that it wasn't readily indentifiable. If I could halt in the grove of trees and, with a few accurate shots, stop the three, then I could leave my horse and retreat up that brushy draw. From up there, I'd have a good view of all three who were after me. They'd probably assume I was still down in the grove with my horse.

I reached the trees only about a hundred and fifty yards ahead of the three. I was off my horse instantly, saddlebags over my shoulder, rifle in my hands. Whirling and kneeling so that my aim would be steadier, I began firing. One horse went down, hit in the chest. A second of the men howled and dived from his horse. I didn't know where he was hit, but it couldn't have been serious judging from the way he scrambled to the doubtful shelter of a scrubby clump of sagebrush.

The third man reined his horse hard right and tried to gallop out of range. I knew this was my chance. Leaving my horse where he was, and crawling, sometimes on hands and knees, sometimes on my belly where the cover was scarce, I went up the brushy draw. They could see the movement of the brush easily enough if they were looking, but the chances were pretty good they weren't. They probably had their eyes fixed on the place they had seen me last, hoping to get a shot the first time I moved.

I got up the draw for about fifty yards without drawing any fire. From there I watched while the one beside the sagebrush clump deliberately shot my horse. The animal went down kicking. He kicked for nearly five minutes before he finally lay still.

That wanton killing only made me madder than I had been before. But it wasn't yet time for me to start shooting. I wanted them up, good targets as they approached the place they had seen me last. They'd wait a long time, of course, considering the possibility that I was playing possum. But eventually they'd reach the conclusion that I was dead or badly hurt and that it was safe to approach, particularly since, with three guns cocked and ready, they could riddle me before I could possibly get off more than a single shot.

The man behind the brush clump yelled, "Hey, kid! What the hell you shootin' at us for? All we wanted to do was return your horse!"

I didn't reply because doing so would have given my location away. I waited, hardly daring to breathe. I was hunkered down as low as I could get with my rifle shoved out in front of me and resting in a crotch of a limber branch of brush.

The time passed, half an hour of it. One of the men was safely hidden behind the horse I had killed. A second was out of sight behind his clump of brush. The third sat his horse out of effective range. Standing Bear's horse was grazing about a hundred yards farther away.

Another half hour passed. Finally one of the men yelled, "Hell, I think we got him, Luke!"

"Maybe. Go on in there and look."

"Not by myself. I'll go in, but only if both of you come too!"

Nothing more was said for another ten minutes. Then finally the man on the horse approached. He reached the other two and they stood up. They stared uncertainly at the spot where my dead horse lay. They talked briefly among themselves, but in tones not loud enough for me to understand. Finally the one on the horse said, "Hell, come on. That kid had a lot of gold in them saddlebags. I'd bet on it."

The three started toward the grove of trees. I let them get to within about twenty-five or thirty feet of it, let their confidence grow and their vigilance relax.

Then I drew a bead on the man on horseback, on the middle of his chest. I'd thought I would be shaking but I was steady as a rock. I fired and I didn't even wait to see what happened to the man. I jacked another cartridge in, shifted my aim to the next man and fired a second time. This one went a little low, and I figured it might have got him in the belly. But I didn't wait to see. I shifted my aim again.

The third man had turned and was running away. I hesitated only a moment, hating to shoot anybody in the back. Then I realized if I didn't, he'd be after me until either he killed me or I killed him. I fired and saw him too go down.

I didn't know whether all three were dead and I didn't care. I had no intention of sticking around and letting them kill me while I tried to help them.

I got up, climbed out of the brushy ravine, and headed straight down the side of the bluff. I circled the three men on the ground, and their horses, and headed for Standing Bear's horse.

I hadn't exactly been keeping count, but I had killed a lot of men. By the time I was twenty-one, if things kept going this way, I'd have killed more men than Billy the Kid.

Only with me there was a difference. I hadn't killed anybody who wasn't trying to kill me. And except for that one man, running away, I hadn't shot anybody in the back.

What bothered me was that I couldn't see an end to it. Even if everybody else left me alone, there was still Rafe and Standing Bear.

Chapter XIII

At least, I now had Standing Bear's horse back and he was a lot better than the one that had just been killed. I hesitated for several moments, staring back toward the northeast to make sure Rafe and Standing Bear were not yet in sight.

I had a choice. I could head back home. I wasn't sure I could find it, since a lot of my traveling had been done at night and a lot of the time I hadn't been paying attention to landmarks. But I knew its general location and could find the town of Halliday easily enough by making inquiries. The trouble was, I wasn't going to be any safer at home than I had been before. Less safe, maybe, because Rafe would see to it that the law came after me for the men I had killed. The killings had been strictly in self-defense, but I'd have to prove it, and in the meantime I'd be in jail. If Rafe could get me hanged legally, it would relieve him of the need of killing me himself.

The other choice was to continue on to Denver, and this alternative appealed to me the most. For one thing, I wanted to keep my promise to Susan Overman. For another, I thought there was a fair chance of losing Standing Bear and Rafe in a city of Denver's size.

For now, my best chance of losing Standing Bear lay in

the tree-lined bed of the Platte River, about three miles on my left. I headed that way.

I had an inherent advantage in that I could travel faster than Standing Bear and Rafe could, even when my trail was fairly plain. But I had lost two hours ambushing the men who were chasing me, and that two hours might be critical in the end. But Standing Bear's horse seemed fairly fresh, so I urged him into a lope, keeping a watchful eye on the road that stretched away to my right. Once, I thought I saw a lift of dust, but I didn't see it again and finally decided I had imagined it.

Reaching the wide, tree-lined Platte River bottom, I rode immediately to the stream, which here ran about a hundred yards wide and shallow enough in most places to see the bottom. I put Standing Bear's horse into it at an angle that would indicate I intended to go downstream. That would probably make Standing Bear feel he had to check out the chance that I had headed back toward home instead of toward Denver. Even if he did not believe that was what I had done, the checking would cost him time.

Almost immediately, I turned and headed back upstream. Standing Bear's horse seemed to enjoy the coolness of the water, and several times he stopped and pawed the water violently enough to splash it over both him and me. I didn't try to stop him because I knew that anything that made him feel better was bound to help me too.

All the rest of the day I stayed in the water, and when I came out, I did it at a place where dead leaves and grass were thick and would not leave too noticeable a trail.

I didn't dare build a fire, but the gunnysack of supplies I'd gotten at the stage depot was still tied to the saddle, and now I dug into it to see what there was to eat.

There was cold meat, biscuits, bacon and potatoes. I ate several biscuits and some of the cold meat, which tasted like antelope. I didn't have blankets, but I had Standing Bear's saddle blanket, and I covered myself with it when I lay down to sleep. I let the horse graze, but I tied the picket rope to my ankle instead of to the stake. My rifle lay at my side, fully loaded, and the revolver was in my hand when I went to sleep.

I awoke at first light. The horse was still there and so were both my guns, my saddle and saddlebags. I got up immediately, got some more biscuits and cold meat out of the sack, then mounted and rode back into the river.

All day I maintained a steady trot. The horse seemed to enjoy traveling in the shallow water, and splashing the water onto his belly and sides. The Rockies, straight west of me, grew ever larger, and in the morning's clear air I could see something I had never seen in my life before. White patches of snow on the highest peaks, even though it was early August, when I had thought all the snow should have been gone. The river changed direction gradually as I rode. Instead of coming from a southwesterly direction, it now came from almost directly south.

At times the stage road was visible. There was a lot more traffic on it now—wagons, horsemen and an occasional mud wagon that probably carried passengers between Denver and some of the smaller settlements. In early afternoon, I saw a big Concord coach go by.

That evening, I figured I would reach Denver on the day following. I also faced the probability that if I encountered Rafe and Standing Bear in Denver, the fight would not be with rifles but with revolvers and at close range. It would be a good idea if I practiced getting the gun out as quickly as I could, and sighting it, so that at least I'd have a chance.

I still wasn't willing to risk a fire, not only because of my fear of Rafe and Standing Bear, but because a fire might draw others like the three who had tried to rob me day before yesterday. So I ate cold meat and finished the biscuits, and then, while my horse grazed, stood self-consciously and practiced drawing the converted Navy Colt, clicking the hammer on an empty cylinder. I was extremely awkward at first, and the gun often caught on the holster so that I had to yank it free. I discovered that there was a place on the holster that caught it every time. With my knife, I pared this part of the holster off.

After that, the gun came out of the holster easily. I kept practicing until it was too dark to see. Then I went to bed, again using the saddle blanket to protect me from the chill.

I lay awake for half an hour, wondering what the future course of my life was going to be. Provided, of course, that Rafe didn't end it within the next few days or weeks.

I'd heard about the famous gunfighters in towns like Wichita, Dodge City, and Tombstone. I'd heard of Billy the Kid, whose tally of dead men was legendary. I knew how these men faced each other in dusty, deserted streets, drawing simultaneously, with the one who was slowest or whose first shot missed, dying in the dust.

Men talked about those things in the bunkhouse, but they really didn't affect any of us. Real cowboys never even carried guns, except for carrying rifles occasionally when they were hunting antelope. A gunfight with handguns was unheard of in our part of the country.

Now it looked like I was about to come to grips with that world of legend that I'd only heard about. Something I did not realize was that, in a sense, I was following in my father's footsteps. Maybe the problems and the antagonists were different but the essentials were the same. I was trying to survive in a hostile world. Which was precisely what my father had been doing when he first built the sod cabin and settled the Halliday Ranch.

I was only sixteen, but I knew one sure danger that I

faced. Rafe would do his best to brand me a killer with whatever law-enforcement officers he encountered, whether they be in Denver or in one of the mining towns in the mountains west of there. Not satisfied to brand me killer, he was certain to tell that I had stolen five hundred dollars and a horse from Standing Bear. There would be an increasing need for me to defend myself or be taken and thrown in jail.

I also knew that if I ever let myself be thrown in jail, it would be the end of me and Rafe would have won. Justice in this part of the country was swift and sure. The penalty for murder or horse stealing was death by hanging. There were no ifs, ands, or buts. If you were found guilty you were hanged. And with Rafe and Standing Bear both testifying against me, there was little chance of me being found innocent even if I was only sixteen years old.

I would have to learn the use of the Navy Colt so that I could get it out of its holster and fire it so swiftly that no one could capture me. I would have to learn to awaken nights at the slightest noise. In short, I would have to learn to live the way an animal does who knows there are predators hunting him.

And for how long? For five long years, unless something happened to Rafe and Standing Bear. Or unless I was able to kill them both.

That wasn't impossible, I thought. What had made it impossible up to now was my awe of both these men. Rafe had been almost like a father to me. My first memories included Rafe, always there, my father's right-hand man and foreman of Halliday Ranch. Standing Bear had come later, but he had been around for six or seven years. He had taught me all I knew about tracking.

Hard as it would be, I was going to have to overcome my awe of both of them. They had forfeited their right to my respect. They were hunting me down like game. Because they wanted the ranch my father had left to me.

This was the way I rationalized. But the truth was, the things I had been forced to do bothered me. I had hunted antelope and occasionally buffalo. I had helped when we slaughtered a steer or hog. So it wasn't the death or the blood that bothered me. It was the taking of human life.

One of the Commandments said, "Thou shalt not kill." And I had killed. Moreover, if things kept going in the future the way they had in the past, I would kill again.

Yet I told myself that my father had killed when he was building Halliday Ranch. He had killed raiding Indians, who would have killed everyone on the ranch if they could, including me. He had hanged two rustlers once before I was old enough to remember anything. And he had shot two horse thieves when they put up a fight instead of surrendering. I wondered how he had felt about being forced to kill. I doubted if he'd wasted much time feeling guilty about it. Maybe one of the Commandments did say, "Thou shalt not kill." But that hadn't stopped David from killing Goliath. It hadn't stopped the men in those ancient times from killing in defense of their lives, in defense of their families or friends, or of their homes. The Bible didn't qualify the Commandments, of course. But I was willing to bet the Lord was going to take circumstances into account when the time came for judging a man.

I tried to put those kinds of thoughts clear out of my head. Doubting myself and the morality of what I was doing was only going to put my life in jeopardy. Doubt would slow me down when circumstances demanded that I be swift.

What I really needed was some help. I needed someone to tell the law officers in Denver what Rafe and Standing Bear were trying to do. But there wasn't anybody. Rose

Moran's voice wouldn't be listened to even if she was there. No one else had actually seen either Rafe or Standing Bear try to take my life. And certainly nobody was going to believe a sixteen-year-old, particularly one who has left a trail of dead men behind him, who has stolen a horse and used the gold out of the saddlebags on that horse. No, if the matter came before the law, I'd be jailed. Rafe might plead for me eloquently enough to get me released into his custody. But I'd never get back to Halliday Ranch alive.

My best hope now lay in losing myself in Denver. I didn't know exactly how big it was, but I'd been hearing about it most of my life. A few of the cowhands on Halliday Ranch had been there, and they'd told stories about how big it was. They'd told about the streetcars and the three-story brick buildings, and the cobblestone-paved streets. And mostly about all the people who were always on the streets, ladies dressed like the one who had been on the stagecoach. Miners. Teamsters. I could hardly wait to see it all.

I kept looking back every time I had a clear view of a long stretch of river, but I didn't see either Rafe or Standing Bear. They were probably at least a full day behind.

The river finally angled toward the west and crossed the road. There was a bridge, only wide enough for a single vehicle at a time. Several were awaiting their turn at either end of the bridge. Horsemen simply rode their horses into the stream, which was belly deep on a horse due to the narrowness of the river here.

I studied the vehicles but I didn't recognize any of them or any of their occupants. I supposed I made a strange sight, armed to the teeth the way I was. As soon as I was out of sight of those waiting at the bridge, I took off my revolver and belt and put them into one of the saddlebags. The rifle, in its saddle boot, wouldn't be noticeable. The revolver would.

I saw the city ahead of me finally. Smoke made a haze over it, smoke that rose from several hundred chimneys and from piles of trash and weeds being burned.

How could I hide best, I asked myself. Well, much as I hated doing it, the first thing I must do was get rid of Standing Bear's horse. He was a dead giveaway and would lead them to me quicker than anything else. If I kept him and stabled him, they'd only have to wait where I'd left him for me to show up again. If I sold him, they'd know I was still in town, and they'd search until they found me. I'd thought I could hide in a place as big as Denver, but now I realized I could not. There were only so many hotels and rooming houses. Two men could check every one of them in a couple of days.

All right, I thought. Make them think you've stayed in Denver by selling the horse. Make them use up a couple of days checking out the rooming houses and hotels.

But don't stay. Hitch a ride on a wagon going west. I knew there were forty or fifty small mining settlements in the Colorado mountains. It would take Rafe and Standing Bear months to check out all of them. And they wouldn't have a trail. Not any more.

Seeing Susan Overman again would have to wait. It was too dangerous, for one thing. For another, the wagon train she and her mother were with probably wouldn't even arrive for several days.

There still was something I couldn't force myself to face just yet. It was the simple truth that Rafe, Standing Bear, and I could not, all three, survive. And that, upon what I did, depended whether it would be me or them who did survive.

The thing I could not yet admit was that, in the end, I was going to have to ambush and kill both Rafe and Standing Bear if I was going to live. Or Rafe at least. There could be no other way.

Maybe when I looked into the barrel of Rafe's gun I'd be able to do what I knew must be done. But right now I couldn't even think about laying a cold-blooded ambush and killing them the way I'd killed the three who had wanted to murder me and steal the gold.

Chapter XIV

I had never in my life seen so many people crowded together. It made the town of Halliday look like a wide place in the road. Literally hundreds of people scurried back and forth like ants. Huge freight wagons rumbled along the dusty streets, most drawn by four mules or oxen, some drawn by as many as six. There were buggies, with well-dressed men and ladies in them; there were horsemen, some looking like cowhands, some like miners, some like gamblers. Everybody seemed intent on getting to some other place as quickly as possible. I rode into the stream of them and just let myself be carried along.

At the first livery stable I came to, I turned and rode up the plank ramp into the fragrant interior which smelled of horses, hay, and dry manure. There was a tackroom at one side of the entrance. I dismounted and approached the man who came out of it. "I want to sell my horse."

He looked the horse over, then glanced at me suspiciously. "Where'd a kid your age get a horse like this? You a runaway? You steal it from your pa?"

"No, sir. I ain't a runaway and the horse belongs to me. See that H Quarter Circle brand on his hip? That's the Halliday brand and my name's Frank Halliday."

"That don't prove nothing. You could still be a runaway and you could still have stolen the horse from your pa."

"No, sir. My father's dead. The horse and the ranch belong to me."

"Why'd you leave it, then? And if you own a ranch, how come you got to sell your saddle horse?"

I was getting tired of arguing with him. I asked, "Do you want to buy him or don't you?"

"I don't. Sure as hell somebody'll come along and lay claim to him, and then I'll be out whatever I paid you for him."

I mounted and rode out of the stable and into the street again. I glanced back once. The man was standing in the doorway, hands on hips, scowling after me.

The next stable was the same and the next one after that. I was greeted with suspicion and both stablemen refused to buy my horse. After leaving the third one, I realized belatedly that I was leaving a trail a fool could follow. Selling the horse would be serving notice to Rafe and Standing Bear that I intended to do one of two things. I either meant to stay in Denver, an unlikely possibility in view of the difficulty of staying hidden, or I meant to go on to the mines in the mountains west of town. They'd give the city of Denver a cursory search, probably enlisting the help of the local law-enforcement officers, and then, when they didn't find me here, they'd head into the mountains to look.

I could probably sell the horse, of course, to someone who wouldn't care whether he was stolen or not. But in trying to deal with that kind of person, I'd be exposing myself to possible robbery at the worst. At best, I'd have to take a fraction of what the horse was worth.

At a Chinese restaurant I stopped, tied my horse and went inside to eat. The food was strange to me, being Chinese, but it was tasty and I was hungry enough to polish it

off in less than ten minutes. I paid the bill, went out and
mounted my horse again.

It was now early afternoon. I found a street that led west
and followed it. Pretty soon I came to the river. There was a
ferry sitting on the gravel bottom on this side of the river.
The traffic—wagons, riders, and pedestrians—were crossing
at a gravel ford where the river widened and was no more
than a foot and a half deep.

I sat my horse on the east side of the river, staring at the
grounded ferry and wondering why anybody had built a
ferry for a river no more than eighteen inches deep. Then it
occurred to me that in the spring when the mountain snows
were melting, the river was probably a lot deeper than it
was right now. A ferry was probably necessary.

A wagon halted beside me and the man on the seat
asked, "Lost, youngster?"

He was a big man, nearly as big as my father had been.
He was clean-shaven, except for a tawny, sweeping mustache. He wore a battered, wide-brimmed hat, a red-and-
black plaid shirt, and canvas pants. He wore low-heeled
miner's boots.

His eyes were as blue as the sky and seemed friendly and
warm. I shook my head. "Just trying to decide where to
go."

"You mean in the mountains?"

"Uh huh."

The bed of his wagon was filled with what looked like
mining machinery. He asked, "Looking for work or looking
for gold?"

"Work, I guess."

"I can use a helper if you don't mind dirtying your
hands. The helper I had is lying back there in Denver drunk
and sick."

I guess I looked a little uncertain. I hadn't expected to be offered a job. He said, "Thirty a month, your meals on the road, and a place to sleep at both ends of the run."

"Where you headed?"

"Leadville."

I nodded suddenly and he said, "All right. Tie your horse on behind and climb up here."

I dismounted, tied my horse behind the wagon and climbed up on the seat. I suddenly had the strangest feeling —almost like my father was here with me. For no reason I could explain, I felt safer than I had since leaving home.

The man asked, "What's your name, son?"

I said, "Frank Halliday." I must have sounded wary because he said, "I'm not going to pry into your personal business. You tell me what you want to and not a damn thing more."

I had a sudden urge to confide in this man, but I controlled it and didn't say anything. We drove in silence across the river. The water came up and lapped at the wagon bed but it didn't get any of the cargo wet. Going out of the river, the wheels sank deep into the loose gravel, so I knew the load was a heavy one. "How long does it take you to get to Leadville?" I asked.

"A week at least. Maybe more if we have any trouble or if it rains."

We came to a fork in the road and took the left one. A little later we came to another one, and again took the one on the left. We were paralleling the river, heading almost directly south. In the distance I could see a snow-covered peak.

The man said, "Guess I didn't tell you my name. It's Spence Frazier. You can call me Spence."

I nodded and pointed to the peak. "That's a big mountain. Does it have a name?"

"Sure does. That's Pike's Peak."

I'd heard about Pike's Peak all my life. Now I was actually seeing it. Spence didn't seem to be much of a talker. We jolted along in companionable silence for an hour or so. All the time, the urge to tell Spence all about myself kept getting stronger and stronger until I couldn't keep silent any more. I said, "I guess you think I'm a runaway."

"None of my business, son. You're maybe sixteen. From the look of you, you've been doing a man's work for quite a spell."

"Yes, sir, I have."

He didn't say anything. The compulsion to tell him about myself was almost irresistible.

I said, "If you're going to hire me, I guess you got a right to know. My pa died several weeks ago. A horse fell with him. He had a big ranch up in Wyoming that he left to me. The trouble was, he made the foreman trustee until I'd be twenty-one, and he put in the will that if I died before I was twenty-one, the whole thing would go to the foreman. So the foreman set out to see to it I never got to be twenty-one."

"You mean he tried to kill you?"

"Yes, sir. First thing, he dropped a rattler down on the haystack I was working on. I didn't get bit, so next thing he did was send me out to check one of the springs. When I got there, I ran into two rustlers and they ambushed me. Before the second one died, he told me he and his friend had been hired to kill me."

"He might have been lying."

"No, sir. Rafe, the foreman, came after me, with a Sioux that breaks horses for the ranch and is a good tracker. Once, when they caught up, Rafe took a couple of shots at me. He's trying to kill me sure enough."

"What about those rustlers? You don't mean to tell me you killed both of them?"

I said, "I was lucky. I got suspicious and dived off my horse just as they opened up."

"But *both* of them?"

I said, "I'm not exactly proud of it." I might have felt a compulsion to confide in Spence, but I decided right then I wasn't going to tell him about any of the other men I'd killed. Rafe and Standing Bear might know, but their knowing probably wouldn't matter in the end, because I was going to be dead or both of them were instead.

Spence was interested in my story now. He asked, "What happened after that?"

"Well, my horse and gun got stolen while I was sound asleep. Then I ran into some Indians and they took me along with them."

"Kidnaped you?"

"No, sir. They were just being friendly. They lost their liking for me, though, after they came on a bunch of buffalo that had been slaughtered for their hides."

"Then what did you do?"

"Well, there was a fight between the Indians and the buffalo hunters. I got a horse and gun from the buffalo hunters' camp."

"Stole them?"

"Yes, sir. I'm afraid so. I guess there's not much excuse, but I knew Rafe and Standing Bear weren't far behind."

"How'd you get that horse back there?"

"That's Standing Bear's. I came on a wagon that was traveling all alone. There was a girl and her mother and a man driving for them. The Indians attacked and one of the horses got killed. I let them use the one I got from the buffalo hunters until they caught up with their wagon train. It was there that Rafe and Standing Bear caught up. I grabbed Standing Bear's horse and got away. That was when Rafe shot at me."

"And you're sure he knew that it was you?"

"He must have. Standing Bear sure did. He knocked Rafe's rifle barrel aside the second time he shot."

"It's incredible!"

I said, "It's the truth."

"I didn't mean I doubted you."

I decided I'd told him all I was going to. If he found part of my story incredible, he'd sure as hell have trouble accepting the whole of it.

We drove in silence for quite a while. Finally, as it began to get dark, he pulled over to the side of the river to make camp. I helped him unhitch the four mules and take the harness off. We staked out two of the mules and let the other two run free. I didn't know what I ought to do with my horse. I asked, "What do you think I ought to do with my horse?"

"Turn him loose. Throw your saddle up on top of the wagon. I doubt if your horse will hang around the mules for very long. He'll probably wander off. Maybe your foreman and the Indian tracker will find him. Maybe somebody will pick him up, or maybe he'll just head for home."

I knew there was very little chance that Standing Bear would be able to pick up the trail of the horse, either in Denver or on the road leaving it. There was too much other traffic both in the city and on the road. The only place they might pick up the trail would be where we'd left the road.

I turned the horse loose and tossed the saddle, blanket, and bridle up on top of the wagon's load. Standing Bear's horse walked away fifty yards or so, then lay down and rolled. He got up, shook himself and trotted to where the mules were staked out. But he didn't seem comfortable with the mules and after a little while he wandered off. That was the last I saw of him.

I helped Spence gather wood and build a fire when we

had a good-sized pile of it. I had some cold meat, but he had bacon and, of all things, half a dozen fresh eggs. He cooked the bacon, then fried the eggs in the grease. It was the second good meal I'd had today, and when I'd finished I discovered I wasn't hungry any more.

We cleaned the pan and tin plates and cups with sand and water at the river's edge. Then Spence got his blankets and made himself a bed between the wagon and the fire. He asked me if I needed a blanket, but I said no. I could use the saddle blanket the way I'd been doing right along.

I got my saddlebags off the saddle and lay down across the fire from Spence, using the saddlebags for a pillow and pulling the smelly saddle blanket over me. I stared across the fire at Spence.

His eyes were closed. He was breathing regularly. I closed my own eyes but I couldn't go to sleep. I had grown suspicious of everybody and I didn't like the feeling. I made a determined effort to sleep but it didn't work. Finally, feeling like a fool, I stealthily withdrew my revolver from the saddlebag and, with it in my hand, tried again to go to sleep.

I made myself forget all those who had hunted me, ambushed me, stolen from me. I thought instead of those who had helped me—the Indians, Susan Overman and her mother, Spence. Finally I managed to go to sleep.

I wakened several times during the night because of some noise the mules had made, or a coyote yipping on a ridge. I wasn't exactly rested when morning came.

I had learned one thing. I could trust Spence. He had no intention of victimizing or robbing me. In fact, I had a feeling now that when trouble caught up with me, Spence might even help.

We harnessed the mules and hitched them up. We killed our morning fire and climbed to the wagon seat. And the second day of our haul to Leadville began.

Chapter XV

As we drove onto the road from the place we'd camped, I looked back to see if Standing Bear's horse was anywhere in sight. He was not. He'd been ridden pretty hard since he'd left Wyoming and he was probably content to just graze and rest.

After a while the road turned west into the foothills following a small winding stream. It was a one-way road, rocky and rough, and whenever we met another wagon there would be a lot of backing and maneuvering and cursing at mules before the two got past each other. The wagons coming toward us were mostly empty and their drivers gave the right-of-way to Spence's heavily loaded wagon cheerfully.

The canyon road eventually gave way to a shelf road high above the stream. It scared me to look down, but it didn't seem to bother Spence. Once, when we passed another wagon, the other wagon's wheels were less than six inches from the drop.

Spence sat comfortably, hunched forward with his elbows on his knees. After a while he pulled a pipe and tobacco from his pocket and handed the reins to me. I was a pretty good teamster but I'd never driven roads like this before.

Only faintly could I hear the stream roaring in the canyon far below as it tumbled over the rocks.

Spence lighted his pipe. By the time he had finished it, we had left the shelf road and were again traveling beside the stream. At noon, Spence pulled off the road. We unhitched the mules, but did not remove the harness. We led them to water and then let them graze. Spence built a fire and made coffee. I got out my sack of grub and we finished what was left in it.

After that, Spence lay back and stared at the puffy clouds floating in the sky. High on the rocky slopes there were aspen trees that were already turning gold. Spence said, "We'll run into snow before we get to Leadville this trip."

Coming from Wyoming, snow was certainly no stranger to me, although we never had it this early in the year. I was getting curious about Spence. I asked, "You got a family in Leadville, Spence?"

The change in his expression was hardly noticeable but it was there. He was silent for a time and he didn't look at me when he replied. "Had one, son. Wife and a boy a couple or three years younger than you. Had a nice, tight cabin in a place I thought was safe."

I hated to ask what had happened, but I had come this far and I couldn't go back now. Not without seeming not to care. I said, "Thought was safe?"

Now his face actually twisted as if with pain. He nodded. "Snowslide—avalanche came down last winter while I was making a haul from Denver. Tore up trees as thick as my body in a swath two hundred and fifty yards wide. Took the cabin like it was built of matchsticks." He stopped talking, his jaws clenched tight, his eyes unexpectedly bright. "Didn't find their bodies until this spring. They were buried that deep in snow. Six men dug for five days before they finally gave up."

I said awkwardly, "I'm sorry. I shouldn't have asked."

He looked at me. "That's all right. Maybe it's good for me to talk about it." He turned his head and looked at me. "How about you? From the sound of it, you haven't got any family either."

"No, sir. Pa was the last. But there's Dolores, who takes care of the house. And there's Rose Moran." I suddenly wondered just how I was going to explain Rose Moran. I said, "She's got a house on forty acres of land right in the middle of the ranch."

Spence didn't ask what she was doing there or what her relationship was to me. I was grateful for that. Instead he asked, "How big is your ranch?"

I was a little surprised to realize I didn't know. Neither did I know how many cattle ran on it. Pa had kept the ranch books and I doubted if anyone else had actually known those things. I said, "I don't know how big it is, but I think there's somewhere near fifty thousand cattle on it."

Spence whistled. "No wonder Rafe is trying to get rid of you." He was silent a moment and then he said, "Your father must have trusted him, or he wouldn't have made his will the way he did."

"Rafe's been there nearly as long as the ranch."

"What's he look like? So I'll know if I run into him."

I said, "About my height. Skinny but tough as rawhide. Straight black hair. Eyes set close to his nose. Pointed nose and chin and hollow cheeks."

"And the other one? The Indian?"

"Standing Bear? He's tall, over six feet I guess. And big through the shoulders and chest. He's got a belly. Likely weighs over two hundred pounds. Dark skin. Nose like a hawk's beak."

Spence said, "I'll know 'em. How far back do you think they are?"

I thought about that a little bit. I said, "When I reached Denver I don't think they were even a day behind, and they were that far back only because I stole Standing Bear's horse. He likely got another from someone with that wagon train, but it wouldn't have been a saddle horse. Probably a lightweight wagon horse."

"And you figure they lost some time in Denver?"

"Had to. They wouldn't know but what I'd stayed there, trying to hide among all those people. They'd have gone around to the livery stables to see if I sold the horse." I grinned faintly, thinking about that. I said, "I did try selling him. I tried three stables. Nobody would buy him though, because they thought I'd stolen him. The thing is, if they happen on one of those three stables, then they'll figure I did sell the horse and stayed in town. They'll probably spend a week looking for me before they decide that I'm not there."

"By then we'll be in Leadville."

"You don't haul freight all winter, do you?"

"Nope. I cut firewood when the snow gets too deep on the roads. But I'll be able to make a couple more loads this fall. If we don't get an early, heavy snow."

"Do you always haul machinery?"

"Lord, no. I haul everything imaginable. The next load will be for a man who runs a mercantile store. Everything from flour to hardware, I suppose."

We were still in the canyon when we camped that night. I figured we were making ten or twelve miles a day, and I knew it was over a hundred from Denver to Leadville. I asked, "What do they mine in Leadville? Lead or gold?"

"Started out as a gold camp but never amounted to very much. Then somebody noticed that the red earth the gold came out of was pretty heavy. Turned out to be carbonate of lead, with a good bit of silver mixed in with it. It's a booming place now, but I don't know how long it's going to last."

We rode in silence for a long time after that. Finally Spence asked, "What are you going to do? You can't keep running forever. And you can't go home."

I'd already made up my mind that there was only one thing I could do. Rafe had to die or I did. There could be no other end to it. But I didn't want to sound like a bragging kid and I didn't want to sound like killing didn't mean anything to me. Finally I said, "If he catches up with me, I expect he'll do his best to kill me. And I'll have to do my best to see he don't."

"Suppose you kill him? What happens to the ranch then?"

"Rose Moran becomes the trustee."

"You mentioned her before. Is she a relative?"

I felt my face getting hot. I said, "She was a friend of my pa's."

"Oh." Spence's tone said he understood.

I felt like I had to defend Rose. I said, "It wasn't like you think. She's a fine woman. I don't know why my father never married her. Maybe he thought it would be disloyal to my mother's memory if he did. But it wasn't nothing cheap."

Tonight, Spence made biscuits in a Dutch oven. He cooked some meat from a deer he'd killed on the way to Denver for this load and made gravy to put over the biscuits. It was the best meal I'd had since leaving home and I ate like I was starved. Spence grinned at me. "You haven't been eating too good from the looks of you."

"Pa said I was shooting up too fast to put on much weight. But he figured I'd be as big as him."

"How big is that?"

"He was six feet two. And he weighed two hundred and twenty pounds."

Spence grinned at me. "You'd better start growing pretty soon."

I nodded and returned his grin. I liked Spence and it suddenly occurred to me that I sure wasn't being fair to him. When Rafe and Standing Bear caught up with me Spence would probably try to help and he'd just get himself killed for his pains.

I said, "I don't want you to be in the middle when they catch up with me."

He didn't even turn his head. "Don't you worry about that, youngster."

There was nothing more that I could say. Or do.

We kept toiling ever higher into the mountains, and on the sixth day we went over a high pass and could look down into an incredibly huge, nearly flat area that Spence said was called South Park or "Bayou Salade." We descended into the park, where the road was wider and nearly flat.

Spence stopped early that night and dug out a couple of fishlines and hooks from his tote bag. We caught grasshoppers for bait and cut willow for poles. The way those trout struck every time we dropped a grasshopper in the stream, you'd have thought they were starving. We caught enough for supper and Spence fried them and made more biscuits to go with them.

Next day we reached a couple of declining mining camps, Tarryall and Fairplay, and stayed that night beside the river just outside the sprawling, untidy town of Fairplay.

Spence went into town after supper. I stayed at our camp, not only because I didn't want to take a chance that Rafe might be in town, but also to guard our mules. Spence said there was a lot of stealing in these mining camps. He said the miners dealt harshly with it when they caught the thieves, but that they had to catch them first.

He came back about midnight with whiskey on his breath. He went right to sleep and I tried to sleep, but it was a light, uneasy sleep from which I awakened at every little noise.

Next day we toiled up the steepest road that I had seen so far. Spence said it was called Mosquito Pass, and that Leadville was on the other side of it.

Near noon, while we were still short of the summit, it clouded up and began to snow. It grew colder almost immediately. Spence got his heavy sheepskin coat out from under the canvas and offered it to me, but I refused to put it on. After that, he got his blankets out and I wrapped myself in them.

The sleet came first, small frozen pellets that stung when they hit us in the face. In minutes the ground was covered to a depth of half an inch or so. Then the snow began, and it wasn't long before the visibility had dropped to less than a hundred yards.

I don't know how we'd have made it without the mules. But they seemed to have no trouble seeing the road, or else they just knew where it was.

In a ground cover of six inches of snow we pulled into Leadville at dusk. Spence drove the wagon to one of the mills that towered ghostlike in the driving curtain of snow. He drove into a building and left it for the millworkers to unload first thing tomorrow. The two of us took the teams of mules to a stable that belonged to the mill, where we unharnessed them, put them in stalls, and gave them hay. Spence said we'd come back for the wagon and mules tomorrow.

I took my saddle and, walking, we went down the hill. Even if Rafe and Standing Bear were here, I thought, they weren't going to spot me in this blowing snow.

Spence had built himself another cabin, this time on a knoll that overlooked the town. Water had to be carried up to it, but there was no chance of another avalanche taking it.

It was bitter cold inside, but it warmed up quickly after Spence built a fire in the stove.

I asked, "When will you leave for Denver to pick up your next load?"

"Depends on the snow, I guess. If it's not too deep in the morning we'll leave tomorrow."

I was thinking that Susan Overman should be in Denver by the time we got back to it. I was pretty excited at the thought of seeing her and I doubted if I'd have much trouble finding her.

Chapter XVI

It stopped snowing sometime during the night. When morning came, the sky was blue and the sun was bright and before long water began to drip from the eaves.

Spence had an old plaid coat and some blankets he gave me in case we ran into another storm. I left my saddle and saddlebags behind in the cabin, but I got the small sack of gold out and put it into my pocket. I also strapped the revolver on, even though I felt a little foolish doing it.

We walked down the hill and waited outside the Leadville Mercantile until its owner came to open up. He was a thin, bearded man named Rosenstein. Spence got a sheaf of orders from him and we went out and headed for the mill, where we'd left the wagon and teams. We hitched them to the wagon and then drove back to Spence's place. There was a good-sized log stable out back. In the stable were four fresh mules that had been fed and reshod by a blacksmith while Spence had been gone. We took the harness off the tired mules, put it on the fresh ones, hitched up and drove away, taking the steep road leading up to Mosquito Pass.

I was tense and alert as we drove toward Denver. I knew we might meet Rafe and Standing Bear at any time.

Spence said, "You could've stayed behind."

I said, "Hiding only puts it off. Sooner or later I've got to come face-to-face with him. Besides, there's someone in Denver I want to see."

He grinned. "The way you say that makes it sound like a girl."

"It *is* a girl. She's with that wagon train."

"How do you expect to find her?"

"I figure the wagon train would've camped by the river awhile to give the people time to decide what they want to do."

"Does your friend and her folks know what they want to do?"

"It's just her mother. And a man named Kroeger who drives for them. No, they don't know what they want to do." I didn't tell him that I'd asked Susan to marry me or that she had accepted. I figured he might laugh. Or grin at me with tolerance, which would be as bad. When you're sixteen and between being a man and a boy you tend to be a little touchy about people laughing at you. Besides, I was beginning to have some doubts. Susan had agreed to marry me but she might have changed her mind. Or her mother might refuse permission when the time came for it.

In any case, nothing could come of it so long as Rafe was hunting me.

The road was slushy and muddy underneath the slush, but not particularly slick. I wondered what it would be like when it froze. Impassable, I supposed. We reached Fairplay in the afternoon and went on for several miles before we stopped for the night. We were making much better time with an empty wagon than we had with a loaded one, and besides, most of the distance we had to cover was downhill.

The storm had been rain at the lower elevations and by the second day the roads were dry. We retraced our previous route along the stream and finally, five days later, reached Denver on the Platte.

We arrived in the middle of the afternoon. Spence said, "We can get loaded before dark. Then we can drive down to the river bottom and camp. Maybe you can find your friends yet tonight."

I was wary and jumpy as we drove into town. I kept looking to right and left, for Rafe and Standing Bear. Rafe wouldn't hesitate to kill me from the shelter of an alley if he thought he could get away with it. He'd been chasing me for weeks and he must be frustrated and furious over his failure to get rid of me. I held my Spencer rifle across my knees, left hand on the stock, right hand on the receiver with my finger through the trigger guard. A couple of times Spence looked at me. I guess he saw how nervous and jumpy I was because his own glance began searching the faces of those walking the street and probing each alley mouth we passed. Finally he said, "You watch your side, Frank, and I'll watch mine."

That simplified things. But neither of us saw anything and we reached the wholesale warehouse without incident. Spence went in to turn over his sheaf of orders while I backed the wagon up to the dock. The warehousemen got things together quickly and we began loading almost at once.

We finished in about an hour. Spence took great care lashing the canvas over the load because much of it would be damaged if it got wet. Finally we drove away from the dock and headed west again.

Spence said, "I know where there's a regular camp for wagon trains. You want to try that first?"

I nodded and he headed the wagon toward Ferry Street. Spence stood up while he drove across the river, looking for the most shallow place so that the water wouldn't get up to the wagon bed. We got across without getting anything wet and he headed north.

Once, as we drove, he showed me what was left of an Indian camp. He said Arapahos had sometimes camped along the Platte west of Denver, but not so much in recent years because of the slaughter at Sand Creek.

It gave me the willies knowing that Rafe and Standing Bear were most likely nearby. I felt like a target sitting up so high on the wagon seat. There was no telling where Rafe and Standing Bear might be. They could be anywhere. In that thick grove of trees on our right. Below that cutbank up ahead. Rafe might even now have his sights on me.

Thinking that way made me want to jump off the wagon seat. But I controlled myself.

We came around a bend in the river and I could see about fifty canvas-topped wagons up ahead. They were halted haphazardly, but most of them were headed north, indicating that they had arrived from the same direction we had. Spence halted his wagon at the edge of the group and said, "Go ahead, Frank. See if you can find them. I'll get some firewood and unhitch the mules."

I got down and walked among the wagons. Everybody looked curiously at me, probably because I was carrying both a rifle and revolver and because I was so young. I had gone two thirds the way through the group when I spotted the Overmans' wagon. It still had traces of red paint on the bed, and the canvas was torn and mended with a piece of somebody's blue overalls.

A fire was burning beside it and Kroeger was squatting by the fire. I said, "Howdy."

He jumped as if I had really startled him. He said, "Oh, it's you."

"Where's Mrs. Overman? And Susan?"

"In the wagon."

They had heard my voice. Susan jumped to the ground

first and ran to me. She threw her arms around my neck and kissed me on the mouth.

I was pretty embarrassed because Mrs. Overman was climbing out of the wagon and she saw all of it. I held Susan off and said, "Hello, Mrs. Overman."

"Hello, Frank." She was friendly, but I could tell the way Susan had greeted me bothered her.

Susan said excitedly, "I was so frightened when that man shot at you. They went after you as soon as they could, but it took them a while to buy a horse, and the one they got wasn't very fast. I guess they didn't catch up with you or you wouldn't be here now."

I said, "They didn't catch up with me. But I've got a feeling they aren't very far away."

"What are you going to do?"

"I'm working for a freighter. He hauls freight from Denver to Leadville. He's back there at the edge of this camp right now. I want you to meet him."

"We'd like to," said Mrs. Overman.

To Susan I said, "Come on. Walk over there with me."

She agreed excitedly. Mrs. Overman's expression was reserved as if she didn't entirely approve. I felt sure Susan had told her my story, but she probably didn't believe all of it. I had to admit it sounded pretty unbelievable. Like the kind of story some kid would think up to impress those he told it to.

Susan hung onto my arm. When we were out of her mother's hearing she said, "I wasn't sure I'd ever see you again."

I said, "You needn't have worried about that."

She was silent for several moments and then she asked, "Frank, are you sure?"

"About you and me? Of course I'm sure."

"We've known each other for such a short time."

"You having doubts?"

"No. But I know what Mother's going to say when we tell her."

"You haven't told her, then?"

"I couldn't. I wasn't even sure I'd see you again."

I said, "I'll tell her, then."

"Wait a little while. At least not tonight."

I guessed maybe she was right. No use stirring up a storm when I didn't even know I'd be alive when the time for the ceremony came. Besides, the longer we had known each other when we did finally tell Mrs. Overman, the more likely she would be to accept it gracefully.

We reached Spence's camp. He had unharnessed the mules and staked a couple of them out where there was some grass. He had built a fire. I said, "Spence, this is Susan Overman. Susan, Spence Frazier."

Spence looked at her approvingly. "I'm pleased to meet you, Susan."

"Thank you, Mr. Frazier. Frank wants you to meet my mother."

"Sure. Be glad to." He left the fire immediately and we walked back toward the Overmans' wagon. On the way, he asked, "You youngsters known each other very long?"

I wished he wouldn't call me a youngster, but I knew he meant no harm.

"Not very," Susan said. "But long enough to know we like each other."

Spence glanced at me and his eyes were penetrating and questioning. I didn't say anything and after a moment he looked away again.

We reached the Overmans' wagon and I introduced Spence to Mrs. Overman and to Kroeger. Spence seemed a little curt with Kroeger, but he obviously liked Mrs. Overman very much. She invited us for supper and Spence accepted. He stood close to the fire and talked to her while Kroeger squatted not far away and scowled. The way he and Mrs. Overman talked, you'd have thought they'd known each other for years. She told him about her home back east and the trip west, including me finding them and helping them fight off the Indians and afterward letting them use my horse. She told him about Rafe shooting at me.

Spence in turn told her about the cabin he'd had in Leadville and about the avalanche that wiped it out and killed his wife and son. They were so busy talking to each other that they didn't seem to notice Susan and me. Finally I said, "Hadn't I ought to go check the wagon and the mules."

"Yeah. That sounds like a good idea."

Susan and I left and walked toward the place where Spence had left his loaded wagon and his mules. I didn't figure Rafe would be looking for me in a wagon camp because a wagon camp was what he'd chased me away from a couple of weeks before. But I kept a sharp lookout all the same.

The mules were grazing peacefully and the wagon had not been touched. The fire had died down, so I built it up again. We started back.

Susan asked, "Aren't you going to kiss me, Frank?"

I'd been wanting to but I hadn't known just how to go about it. I put my arms around her and kissed her. She was warm and soft and her kiss stirred things in me that I'd never felt before except that once. I pulled away, not wanting to compare Susan with Mary Jane Meier, because there just wasn't any comparison. She asked, "What's the matter?"

"Nothing."

"You're not sorry?"

"Of course I'm not sorry. It's just that . . . well, I guess I just want more."

She laughed softly. "And Spence called you 'youngster.'"

I suddenly felt a sharp stab of jealousy. I asked, "You sound like you knew . . . I mean, have you ever . . . ?"

She was very serious as she said, "No, Frank. But that doesn't mean I don't know anything."

I believed her and I felt better, but I knew we were treading on dangerous ground. I said, "We'd better get on back. Your ma will have supper on."

We started back, with Susan hugging my arm as we walked. If I'd had any doubts before about whether we were old enough, they were gone now. All I had to do was get Rafe off of me and we could go back home to Halliday Ranch. We could get married in Denver before we left.

Spence and Mrs. Overman were still talking when we got back. Mrs. Overman was saying she hadn't yet decided what they would do. Spence said, "Why don't you come to Leadville? It's really booming now."

"What would I do?"

Spence thought about that a moment. "Open a bakery. Bread's selling for a dollar a loaf. I could freight your supplies from Denver."

Mrs. Overman thought about that while she filled the plates. I sat at the fire beside Susan. Spence poured the coffee.

Finally Mrs. Overman looked at Susan. "What would you think of doing that?"

"I think it's a good idea."

Mrs. Overman looked at Spence. "We'll do it, then. We can go to Leadville with you tomorrow."

Kroeger spoke for the first time. "Don't figure me in on that. I ain't going to spend the winter in a place that cold."

Nobody tried to change his mind. I got the feeling both Susan and her mother would be glad to be rid of him. I said, "I can drive for you. If it's all right with Spence."

That was the way we settled it. After supper, Spence and

I returned to our camp. I was to go to the Overmans' wagon first thing in the morning and hitch up their horses. Spence seemed to think the two horses could pull the Overmans' wagon. If we reached a particularly steep place where they had trouble, we could always use two of the mules.

I was so happy at the prospect of seeing Susan every day that for a little while I forgot about Rafe and Standing Bear.

Chapter XVII

Next morning, I helped Spence hitch up the mules. Then I walked to the Overmans' wagon and hitched up their horses. Kroeger had gone. When everything was ready, the three of us climbed to the seat and I drove to where Spence was waiting for us. Spence went first, since his wagon was more heavily loaded. I followed along behind. Mrs. Overman joined Spence on the seat of his wagon after he suggested it. Her face was a little flushed as she did so.

Susan said, "Mother likes your friend."

"Looks like it. Looks like he feels the same way about her."

We returned to the road and Spence turned into it. The route was familiar to me now.

Susan seemed preoccupied and finally I asked, "Something bothering you?"

She turned her head and looked at me. "It's Kroeger. I think he's capable of hunting up those two who are trying to kill you and telling them where you've gone. For a price, of course. I'm sorry. I feel responsible."

"They'd find me sooner or later anyway. Besides, he may not be able to find them."

It was wonderful jolting along on that wagon seat with Susan hour after hour. We talked almost constantly. She told me all about her life and I told her about mine. We talked about things we saw along the way. I told her what Leadville was like, and what Halliday Ranch was like. She seemed fascinated by my talk about the ranch. I said, "You'll like it," and she said, "I know I will."

"You didn't tell your mother last night, did you?"

She shook her head guiltily.

I said, "But she suspects, doesn't she?"

"I'm sure she does."

"What if she says no?"

She was silent for a while, her brow furrowed with worry. Finally she turned her head and looked straight into my eyes. "I'll go with you anyway. But I hope she doesn't."

I squeezed her hand. Up ahead Spence made a sharp turn in the road. Susan's mother was chattering away and Spence was smiling down at her.

The day passed swiftly, and the day after that, and almost before I knew it we were descending Mosquito Pass into Leadville at its foot. Spence drove straight to his cabin. While I unharnessed the Overmans' horses and put them into the stable, he went into the cabin and built a fire. Mrs. Overman and Susan said they'd get supper while Spence and I drove the wagon downtown and unloaded it.

It was the first chance I'd had to talk to Spence alone. He looked at me and grinned. "You got that woman worried, Frank. She figures you and that girl are going to run off."

"We're not going to run off. We're going to ask."

"You're kind of young."

"I am, maybe, but Susan's not. Lots of girls get married when they're sixteen, and I figure if I don't grab her now she might marry someone else."

He studied me a moment. Finally he said, "I don't think you're too young. I think you can handle it."

That made me feel good. I hadn't had any doubts myself, but it helped to have Spence agree with me.

It had snowed again while we'd been gone and this one hadn't melted off so fast. It still lay on the north slopes and on the north sides of the buildings. The streets were muddy and at this time of day crowded with prospectors and miners heading for the saloons and restaurants. We reached the store, drove around into the alley, and backed the wagon up to the dock. I got up on the dock and Spence handed the boxes up to me. I carried them inside and put them where Mr. Rosenstein told me to. When we got to the barrels, I got into the wagon and helped Spence roll them out. After everything was unloaded, I folded the canvas while Spence went into the store to settle up.

I had to force myself to think of Rafe and Standing Bear. I knew that if I didn't think about them, if I wasn't on guard all the time, they'd take me by surprise when they finally did catch up with me. I'd have to get my head out of the clouds or I'd end up dead.

Spence came out and we drove toward his cabin. I was on guard, looking at every man on the street, searching each alley mouth.

Spence was looking for something else, and finally he saw what he was looking for. "There," he said, pointing at an empty store with a "For Rent" sign in the window. "There's a place she can use."

"For the bakery?"

"Yeah. It's big enough so they can live in back, and stout enough to keep out the winter cold."

When we reached Spence's cabin, Mrs. Overman and Susan had supper on. We ate, and afterward we all walked down to the empty store. The owner's name was printed in small letters on the sign. While Mrs. Overman, Susan, and I waited, Spence went to find the man.

When the owner arrived with the key, we went inside. There was a lantern just inside the door and Spence lighted it.

The place was dirty and bare, but that didn't seem to dismay Mrs. Overman. She carried the lantern to the rear, which was partitioned off. Turning, she asked the man how much was the rent.

When he told her, she said without hesitation, "I'll take it." She paid him the first month's rent.

We stayed there half an hour or so while Mrs. Overman made a list of all the things she was going to need. They couldn't be bought in Leadville, Spence told her, because things were too expensive here. He said he and I would go to Denver and bring back everything.

I didn't see how a bakery could fail in a place like this and neither could Mrs. Overman. The bread that Rosenstein sold in his store for a dollar a loaf was stale and sometimes moldy. Fresh bread was bound to be in demand no matter what the price.

We returned to Spence's cabin. Susan and her mother slept in the cabin. Spence and I slept in the stable, which was built of logs and which was reasonably warm from the animal heat of the eight mules and two horses. Next morning Mrs. Overman had her list made up. She gave it to Spence along with money to buy the supplies. We harnessed the mules and as soon as possible left for Denver. Mrs. Overman and Susan said they would spend the time we were gone cleaning the bakery building and getting it ready to occupy. Susan kissed me goodbye in front of her mother, who frowned faintly when she did.

Driving up the steep hill toward the pass, Spence said, "You've got a selling job ahead of you."

I knew he was right. Susan had said she'd go with me

even if her mother refused permission, but I didn't want it that way and I knew Susan didn't either.

I forced myself to think of Rafe. I was surprised that he hadn't already found me. The only explanation I could think of was that there were probably fifty mining camps within a hundred miles of Denver. It would have taken him a long time to check them all.

I found myself wondering how they were getting along on the ranch. Father was gone, and Rafe, and me. I supposed Rafe had made somebody foreman in his absence, so things were probably going along all right. Rose Moran would be worried sick that Rafe would catch up with me, if she realized he was hunting me, but the amount of time that had passed must have been encouraging to her. She would probably reason that the longer I managed to stay away from Rafe, the better my chances of eluding him permanently.

But I couldn't elude him permanently. He was too stubborn. Furthermore, it wasn't only Rafe I had to worry about. Standing Bear might have knocked Rafe's rifle aside and saved my life once. He wouldn't do it again. Rafe would have offered him enough money to make sure he did not. Or he would have threatened him. Or both.

The trip to Denver was uneventful. The aspen leaves in the high country were a brilliant yellow. Nights were cold, and many times we awoke to find frost thick and heavy on everything. It might be a month before winter came to Halliday Ranch, but it could come to this high country anytime.

We reached Denver and located all the things Mrs. Overman had said she'd need. A stove, big and heavy and made of cast iron. Flour. Lard and a dozen other things. Baking pans. It took three days to locate and buy everything. Then we started back.

By that time I was pretty well satisfied that Rafe and Standing Bear were not in Denver. I knew, though, that they hadn't given up. Rafe wouldn't go back to Halliday Ranch until I was dead and until it belonged to him.

Halfway to Leadville, we had a chance to kill a deer. We dressed it out and threw it up on top of the wagon load. Three days later we drove down the steep road off Mosquito Pass and into Leadville once again.

We drove straight to the building Mrs. Overman had rented for her bakery. It was already dark when we arrived, but there was a lamp burning inside. The door was locked.

Spence pounded on the door. Susan and her mother were working in the partitioned-off room in the rear. When they heard the pounding on the door, they both came hurrying to the front. Mrs. Overman unlocked the door and we went in.

I was shocked at their appearance. Both women had ugly bruises on their faces. One of Mrs. Overman's eyes was black. Both of them moved as if each movement hurt.

Neither Spence nor I had to guess what had happened to them. While we'd been gone, Rafe had located them. Knowing I'd been with them in that wagon-train camp out on the prairie where he'd shot at me, he'd assumed I still was with them or that they knew where I was.

Looking at Susan, I could feel fury rising in me. My skin felt hot and both my hands and knees trembled. I asked, "Rafe?"

She nodded mutely, tears suddenly filling her eyes and running down across her cheeks. I held out my arms and she came to them, now weeping almost hysterically.

Mrs. Overman, though even more badly beaten than Susan was, managed to hold onto her composure. I glanced at Spence over Susan's head and his eyes were hot with rage. He asked, "When?"

"Last night. We were just finishing up and heading for your place. They forced their way in and dragged us behind that partition after first locking the door. We both screamed, but I guess these walls are too thick. Then they began asking where Frank was. We both said we didn't know, but they didn't believe. They began hitting us, trying to make us tell them where Frank was."

I could see the same question in Spence's eyes that I knew was in mine. He hesitated a long time, but finally he asked, "Did you tell them?"

Mutely she shook her head.

I felt my throat choke up and for several moments I couldn't have said anything if I'd tried. They could have saved themselves a lot of pain by telling, but they hadn't done so. They'd gritted their teeth and taken all that Rafe handed out.

My arms tightened around Susan. I said softly, "You should have told them."

Mrs. Overman glanced at me. "And had them waiting for you when you returned?"

I decided right then that I'd been running from Rafe and Standing Bear long enough. Tomorrow I was going to go hunting them. Meeting eventually with Rafe was inevitable anyway. And maybe if I was the hunter instead of the hunted, I'd have a better chance.

Besides, I was angry now, more angry than I'd ever been about anything. I intended to make sure that nothing like this ever happened to Susan and her mother again, or to anyone who tried to see that I stayed alive.

Susan's mother apparently decided we'd dwelt on this subject long enough. She said, "Come see what we've done."

I glanced at Spence over Susan's head as I released her. I saw in Spence's face the same determination and anger I felt myself. But I didn't intend to let Spence get himself killed fighting my fight for me. I was going to handle Rafe and Standing Bear alone.

I don't know where Mrs. Overman had found all the things she had in the little room behind the bakery. Some had undoubtedly been in her wagon. But she had fixed up very attractive and livable quarters for Susan and herself.

Spence and I went back out front and began unloading the wagon and carrying the things inside. Every minute I was outside I had the feeling that I was being watched, that someone was out in the darkness aiming a rifle at my head. But no shots were fired and eventually the wagon was unloaded.

I looked at Spence. "You go on home. I'm going to stay here in the bakery tonight."

He nodded, making no protest. I got my blankets. I went back inside and locked the door. Spence drove the wagon away toward home.

I talked with Susan and her mother for a little while. Then I fixed myself a bed on the floor and lay down to sleep. If Rafe and Standing Bear came back, they'd have to go through me before they could get to Susan and her mother again.

And tomorrow . . . tomorrow I was going to go hunting them.

Chapter XVIII

Hard as I tried, I couldn't go to sleep. I kept thinking of Rafe and Standing Bear coming here and Rafe beating both Susan and her mother with his fists while he tried to make them tell where I was.

Another terribly upsetting thought came to me. Susan and her mother were witnesses to his attempt to kill me when I stole Standing Bear's horse out on the plains. They could testify that he had beaten them both trying to make them tell where I was. If I turned up shot . . . well, Rafe just couldn't afford to let them live to testify against him and to thus deprive him of Halliday Ranch, which he would have murdered me to acquire.

I was alternately hot with anger at what Rafe had done to them, and cold with fear for their safety. I admitted finally that I now had only one alternative. I had to kill Rafe, no matter how I had to do it, before he could kill me and them. Hard as it was to face, it must be faced.

I was aware that I was going to have to proceed with extreme care. Spence had told me that Leadville, after its first wild, lawless year, was now trying to clean up its streets and make them safe for its citizens. The almost nightly killings had become a thing of the past, due to rigid, even harsh law enforcement. Leadville had a marshal in addition to the county sheriff, who made his headquarters here. Both marshal and sheriff had several deputies. When someone broke the law he was marched off to jail. His trial was swift, his punishment predictable. For murder the penalty was death by hanging. The sentence was usually carried out within a week.

So if I killed Rafe, it would have to be done in a way that would not put me in jeopardy with the law.

Rafe would be operating under a similar handicap, though. He too would be held to account by the law if he managed to kill me. Except that I was convinced Rafe could do something I could probably not force myself to do. He could kill in the darkness, from ambush, or shooting from behind. And once he had finished me off, he'd turn his attention to Mrs. Overman and Susan, and to Spence, any one of whom could accuse him of murdering me. Because if he was accused, even if there was not enough evidence to convict him and hang him for the crime, he would certainly have trouble inheriting the ranch.

Another disquieting thought occurred to me. Rafe might, in view of the fact that Spence and the two women knew my story, give up the idea of killing me outright. He might accuse me of killing the two rustlers on the ranch. He and Standing Bear might swear the men were working for the ranch. They would deny I owned the ranch, and the authorities here would probably accept their word, since my story, coming from someone my age, was not very believable.

I could be tried and executed right here. Or I might be turned over to Rafe and Standing Bear to be returned to Wyoming for trial. If I was, I'd never reach Wyoming or even the Colorado line.

Considering this last possibility, I began to feel extremely uneasy about staying here all night. But Susan and her mother were asleep. I couldn't leave them unprotected again.

Slowly, I forced my mind to stop its frantic seeking for some way out. And eventually, long after midnight, I went to sleep.

I was awakened by a pounding on the door. It was light but the sun had not come up. Through the window I could see a group of men outside.

I felt like an animal caught in a trap. I knew there was no back door. There was a window in back, though, and I pulled on my boots, got up and headed around the partition just as Susan and her mother, clutching wrappers around themselves, came through heading the other way.

We collided. I said, "I think it's the law and my guess is they're after me. I'm going out the window in back. Wait just a minute before you open up." I had my rifle, but the revolver lay beside my blankets where I'd been sleeping when the pounding woke me up.

I rushed to the window, knowing I'd have to break it to get out. I never quite got to it. I saw two men outside while I was still six feet away. They'd closed off my escape route. There was no way I could get away.

The pounding now on the front door was harder and a voice bawled, "Open up in there!"

I nodded to Mrs. Overman. She called, "Who is it?"

"The marshal! Open up!"

"Just a minute." She clutched her wrapper around her and unbolted the door. It was opened so violently that it struck her and nearly knocked her down. I dropped my rifle as it did. There was no use getting shot.

Several men burst into the room, guns drawn. One had a star-shaped badge pinned to his shirt. He looked at me and asked, "You Frank Halliday?"

"Yes, sir."

He crossed the room, grabbed me and whirled me around. I didn't resist, because I'd probably get a knot on the head if I did. Besides, there wasn't any use. I felt my arms jerked behind my back and felt a pair of heavy, rusty handcuffs snapped over my wrists.

Mrs. Overman protested, "What is this all about? What do you think he's done?"

"He's killed a man, that's what. Killed him for the gold he had on him." He already had his hand in my pocket and when he drew it out he had the buckskin bag with the gold coins in it. "Here," he said triumphantly. "Here it is."

"When was all this supposed to have taken place?"

"Last night."

"He's been here all night."

"You sure of that? Were you both awake all night?"

Mrs. Overman shook her head. "But we'd have heard him if he'd left."

The marshal shook his head. "I don't doubt you, ma'am, but he could've gotten out of here and come back without you hearing him."

Mrs. Overman now saw Rafe among the men behind the marshal. She said in a voice shrill with near hysteria, "There he is! That's the man who beat my daughter and myself."

The marshal shook his head. "Won't do, ma'am. That's the man who says this kid killed Spence Frazier."

To hear that name spoken after the word "killed" was like a blow in the stomach to me. I could feel the blood draining out of my face, and my heart felt like it was being squeezed. I said feebly, "Spence? Spence is dead?"

"You know damn well he's dead because you killed him last night."

"Why would I kill him? He was my friend. I worked for him."

The marshal opened the buckskin sack and poured the coins out into his palm. "Here's why. Two hundred and forty-seven dollars. That's damn near a year's wages at what he was likely paying you."

I glanced at Rafe. His face was dark and expressionless, but there was a gleam of triumph in his eyes. Standing Bear wasn't here among the other men.

I felt tears come to my eyes at the thought of Spence being dead. I looked at Mrs. Overman and saw tears in her eyes too. Susan was weeping openly. I said, "Mrs. Overman, I haven't left this room all night. I swear to you . . ."

She nodded. "I know you haven't, Frank. It's that man Rafe who killed Spence, just like he tried to kill you that night out on the plains."

The marshal said, "This kid's sure got you fooled, ma'am. He's a bad one, if what this man here says is true. Killed two men in Wyoming. Killed a couple of buffalo hunters this side of the Colorado line. A regular Billy the Kid, he is."

"According to who? Rafe?"

"Yes, ma'am. Rafe's a sheriff's deputy, sent after this kid along with an Indian tracker. Too bad they couldn't have caught up with him last night. Would've saved Spence Frazier's life."

I asked, "You see his credentials?"

"You bet I did. He's a sheriff's deputy right enough. Got the badge to prove it."

Rafe had probably bought a sheriff's badge in Denver while he was there. He'd be that thorough because that was the kind of man he was.

I felt limp and weak. I didn't even feel like trying to defend myself. I was sick at my stomach thinking of Spence lying dead. Because of me. Because he'd befriended me and given me a job and promised to help me when the show-down came.

There was no use trying to tell the marshal where I'd got-ten the gold coins. I'd stolen it from Standing Bear, and ad-mitting that wouldn't help me at all. The marshal gave me a shove. "All right, kid. Head on down toward the jail."

I went through the doorway. Just outside, I turned. "Tell me one thing. How was Spence killed?"

He laughed harshly. "Don't give me that! You know how he was killed. Rammed the gun right up against him so it wouldn't make no noise and then pulled the trigger."

I walked down the hill, prodded occasionally from be-hind by the marshal's gun muzzle. Once he said to one of his deputies, "By God, there's something wrong with kids these days. Way they're raised, I guess. Just imagine, six-teen years old and he's already killed six men. Maybe more that nobody knows about."

At the bottom of the hill I looked back. Rafe was no longer with the group. Mrs. Overman and Susan stood in front of the bakery. I could tell that Susan was still crying.

I wondered where Rafe had gone. I wondered if he'd dare hurt Mrs. Overman and Susan now that he had been accused of beating them. I doubted it. I believed they were safe, at least for now. But after he had disposed of me, if he thought them capable of traveling to Halliday to try and deprive him of the ranch, then they'd be in deadly danger again.

We turned the corner and they were lost to sight. Now I thought of Spence. When I'd first heard he had been killed, I'd been numb with grief. Now I was beginning to feel anger stirring inside of me. And determination. That Rafe wasn't going to get away with this. I didn't know how I'd manage it, but I would. Somehow I'd stop him. Somehow I'd see to it that he paid for killing Spence.

We reached the jail. It was built of stone and, except for the bars on the windows, looked like any of the other square, false-fronted buildings along this street. I guessed it had probably been a store originally and had been converted to contain the jail.

There was a hillside behind it and the rear third of the building was partially dug into the side of the hill. The cells were probably damp and cold, I thought, as the marshal shoved me roughly through the door.

I went through another doorway and into the cell corridor. There were six tiny cells, three on each side of the corridor. All but one were occupied. I was put into the sixth, against the wall at the rear. There was one tiny barred window and through its dirty glass I could see the rocky hillside behind the jail. The sun had come up and now bathed the hillside with its light.

The marshal took the handcuffs off. He unlocked the cell door and pushed me inside. The door clanged shut and the key turned in the lock.

I wouldn't even be allowed to go to Spence's funeral, I thought. I wondered when it would be. Tomorrow, probably. Or the next day at the latest. I knew Spence had a lot of friends in Leadville. Driving down the street he had always spoken to nearly everyone. Besides, nobody could have helped liking Spence.

Rafe must have been watching us last night, I thought. He'd probably watched us unload and carry all the things from the wagon into the bakery. He could have shot me then, I thought, and for a moment I wished to God he had, because if he had, Spence would still be alive.

He'd watched Spence go home. And then the idea had probably occurred to him. He didn't have to kill me himself and risk not inheriting the ranch. He could let the law kill me for him. By killing Spence and blaming it on me, he could get his dirty work done without dirtying his hands.

There was a rusty iron cot in the cell. The floor was wet from moisture that had seeped in from the hillside into which this part of the building was dug. There was a rusty bucket to be used as a chamber pot. A salamander waddled across the floor.

I sat down on the bunk. The other inmates were staring at me curiously through the bars. "What you in for, kid?" one of them asked.

I didn't want to talk, but I didn't want to antagonize anybody either. I said, "For killing a man."

The man whistled. "You're getting an early start."

I said, "I didn't do it."

"Sure. None of us done what we're in here for."

I didn't pursue it any farther. There wasn't any use, and besides, I didn't feel like talking to anyone. I wanted to think. I wanted to try and figure out some way of getting out of here.

But there wasn't any way. I hadn't time to dig my way out, and I had no tools and no way to get rid of the dirt even if I tried. The bars were stout, the lock strong. There was no way of breaking out.

If Spence had still been alive, I'd have had someone working from the outside to get me freed. But Spence was dead. And nobody was going to listen either to Mrs. Overman or Susan. The truth was, nobody was going to help.

It might even be the other way. Spence had lots of friends. They would want his killer to pay the price. They might even try to take the law into their own hands.

That thought made a chill run along my spine. They might try lynching me. This was a wild and, until recently, a lawless town. It was still wild even if there was some law.

I was shivering, partly from the damp and cold, partly

from fear and a feeling of hopelessness. It looked like Rafe
had won. I'd be brought to trial, convicted, and sentenced
to be hanged. Rafe and Standing Bear would stay in Leadville long enough to see the sentence carried out. Then Rafe
would go home and take over that which rightfully was
mine.

(And I couldn't stop it. There wasn't one damn thing that
I could do.) *me*)

Chapter XIX

It couldn't have been much later than eight o'clock when the cell door slammed behind me. The marshal disappeared into his office and closed the door.

I crossed the cell and shoved the bunk under the barred window so that I could climb up and look out. The hillside was about four feet below my window. A man could stand there, break the window, poke a rifle through and kill someone inside with ease. The way the streets were always crowded, he could disappear into the crowd before the marshal or any of his deputies could run around in back.

That discovery made me feel like a duck in a shooting gallery. I climbed down and sat on the cot. The man in the cell next to mine, a huge, bearded man, asked, "What you in here for, kid?"

"Murder. But I didn't do it."

"Sure. None of us done anything. Who you supposed to have killed?"

"Spence Frazier."

"Spence is dead?" There was shock in the big man's voice. A murmur ran through the other cells and it was obvious that some of these men had known Spence and liked him. One said, "You little sonofabitch!"

I said, "I told you I didn't do it. Spence was my friend. I worked for him."

The men began talking among themselves. I couldn't help keeping an eye on the window, even though I knew there was little danger now. Besides, the sound of breaking glass would warn me if I was expecting it.

I thought of Susan and her mother. I knew Susan believed me to be innocent, but I wasn't sure her mother did. What worried me wasn't what they thought of me but the danger I believed them to be in. Rafe had beaten them trying to make them tell him where I was. Their accusation of him had not been believed this morning, since the marshal and sheriff had simply thought they were defending me. But if they pressed it . . . Rafe might think he had to silence them.

I began to wonder who had found Spence's body and how Rafe had justified his accusation of me. I yelled, "Marshal!"

There was so much noise in the cells that he probably didn't hear. I picked up the slop bucket and banged it on the bars. Again I yelled, "Marshal!"

The door opened and he stuck his head through. "Shut up back here!" he shouted.

The other men quieted. I said, "I've got to talk to you."

"You can do your talking in court."

I said, "Please. Who found Spence this morning?"

"That fella that's accusing you. Rafe Joslin."

"And how did he know that I killed Spence?"

"Spence wasn't dead. Talked before he died."

I felt a big empty space where my stomach ought to be. Weakly I asked, "How did Rafe happen to be at Spence's place so early in the morning?"

"Wanted some things freighted from Denver on Spence's next trip."

I felt defeated and discouraged. Rafe had apparently thought of everything. Claiming Spence had named me as his killer just before he died would practically make sure I was convicted of the crime. But I couldn't just give up. I said, "Mrs. Overman and her daughter told you Rafe had beaten them."

"Why would a Wyoming peace officer beat two women? Huh uh. They're just saying that to help you out."

"He's no peace officer."

"He's got the credentials and that's a hell of a lot more than you got, son."

There wasn't anything more I could say that I hadn't already said. He wasn't going to believe me anyway. He had his mind made up that I was another Billy the Kid, and I wasn't likely to change it. When I got into court it would probably be the same. Rafe would be believed and I would not. I'd be found guilty and probably sentenced to be hanged, or, because of my age, sentenced to prison for a long, long time.

The marshal went back into his office and I sat down glumly on the cot. I put my head down in my hands. I could hear a low hum, probably the mingled sounds of activity in the street. It seemed to be getting louder, but I supposed that was because more people were now on the street than had been there earlier.

I hadn't slept much last night and I was tired. I stretched out on the cot and closed my eyes. The other prisoners were talking and the hum of street noises continued to grow.

I guess I fell asleep, though how I could under the circumstances I don't know. I awakened as the door opened between the cells and the marshal's office. The marshal came through into the corridor. He said, "I got a letter for you, kid."

He came toward my cell and I got up and went to the bars. With the office door open, I could hear the street noises more distinctly. That hum had not been street noise.

It was the mingling of many voices. Looking along the corridor and out through the front window, I could see a solid mass of men packed before the jail.

I took the letter. The marshal had opened and read it before bringing it to me. I waited a moment before taking it out of the envelope and asked, "What are all those men doing in front of the jail?"

"They're Spence's friends."

"What do they want?"

"They're just upset." His voice was evasive and he didn't look at me.

I asked, "What time is it?"

He dragged a big silver hunting-case watch from his pocket, opened the cover and said, "Eleven o'clock." He turned and went back into his office, closing the door behind.

I was anxious to read the letter, which I knew had come from Susan, but I couldn't get my mind off the crowd of men in front of the jail. They had been yelling. A few had looked like they were already drunk in spite of the fact that it wasn't even noon. All had looked angry. They were more than just upset.

I thought that from men like those out in the street the jury that decided my fate would be picked.

I sat down on the cot and opened Susan's letter. She said she knew I had not killed Spence. She said she and her mother would do everything they could to get me out. If they weren't able to do that, they'd show up in court and testify.

That last statement scared me. Rafe might not want to risk letting them testify, because there was a chance the court might believe their testimony. They were both very pretty, and pretty women were scarce in a town like this. Somehow I'd have to get word to Susan and her mother and tell them to stay out of it. I couldn't risk letting either of them be hurt.

The man in the cell next to me said, "That's a mob out there, kid. Sounds to me like they're getting madder all the time."

I sat there feeling cold, but the cold wasn't caused by the damp walls and floor of the cell. It was the kind of cold that comes from inside you.

I began to pace back and forth, partly from nervousness, partly trying to drive away the chill. Finally I stopped beside the bars dividing my cell from the next. The big man was watching me. I asked, "What are you in here for?"

"Same thing as you. Only I killed a man in a fight."

"What kind of men are the marshal and the sheriff?"

"You mean, will they fight off a mob?"

I nodded. "I guess that's what I mean."

He said, "Nobody's been lynched in Leadville yet."

"Has it been tried?"

"There was some talk about it six months ago. But they never tried to break into the jail."

I said, "Do you think they'll fight off that mob?"

"I think they'll try."

That was some comfort but not very much. I continued to pace back and forth and the time dragged by. At noon the sheriff and a couple of his deputies brought dinner to all the prisoners. Trays were shoved under the barred doors.

I didn't feel like eating and the food didn't look good, but I forced myself. It helped pass the time and for a few minutes at least it took my mind off what was going to happen to me. When I finished I put the tray beside the door so that the deputies could get it when they returned.

They came in shortly and gathered up the trays. One of them unlocked my cell. "The marshal wants to talk to you."

I couldn't help feeling suspicious but I followed him

along the corridor and into the office. He closed the door behind me.

Outside, men were now packed solid, blocking traffic in the street. The marshal said, "They're getting ugly." I saw that he and the others had shotguns within easy reach.

The marshal was a blocky man, sandy-haired, with a bushy mustache. His eyes were blue. He said, "It's your Wyoming lawman that's stirring those men up and buying drinks. I think maybe it's time I heard your side of this."

I told him, from the time my father died up until right then. I watched him while I talked. At first, his expression was doubting, but as the story went on, he began to look interested and there was less doubt in his face.

Rafe had made a mistake egging on the mob and buying drinks. Maybe he hadn't been willing to risk letting me go to trial. But if he hadn't egged on the mob the marshal would never have had any doubts. Finally the marshal nodded to the deputy who had brought me out. "Take him back. No matter who's telling the truth, we're going to have our hands full before today is over with."

I said, "Could you send a man to guard Mrs. Overman and her daughter? He beat them and if he'd kill Spence just to get me arrested he's not above killing them."

"Can't spare anybody now. But I'll keep an eye on Joslin if that will make you feel any better."

It did. I went back to my cell. I'd thought things were hopeless, but maybe they weren't completely hopeless yet. Even so, I was a long ways from being in the clear.

The mob was still outside and it was almost certain they'd try to storm the jail. The marshal, the sheriff, and their deputies might not be able to hold it. If they weren't . . . I felt sick at my stomach at the thought of being lynched.

And even if I wasn't lynched, I still had to go to trial.

Getting the marshal to believe me wasn't going to be enough. I'd have to get a twelve-man jury to believe me too.

Even if I did and was acquitted and turned loose, there still would be Rafe. It always came back to that.

I told myself that I'd traveled five hundred miles with two determined men hunting me. I'd eluded them for almost three months. I'd had no friends, no allies, and I'd still managed to stay alive.

Now I had Susan and her mother. The marshal seemed to believe in me, at least partially.

I thought of Spence again, who had died for befriending me. If I could stay alive, Rafe was going to pay for killing him.

Chapter XX

That afternoon was the longest I have ever spent. The noise out in the street was a steady, low-pitched roar. I wondered how long that many men could stay stirred up. Probably the mob in front of the jail changed continuously as men left to go into the saloons for drinks and others came out to join the mob. Sooner or later the situation would explode. Probably when it got dark. Mobs operate better in the dark when their faces are not as recognizable as they are in the bright light of day.

Gradually the light in the cells faded. A deputy brought a single lantern and hung it in the corridor.

Not long afterward, I heard the crash of breaking glass and, almost simultaneously, the crash of a battering ram striking the front door of the jail. The howling of the mob rose to a crescendo, and three shotgun blasts boomed out.

I gripped the bars of my cell, trying to ready myself for what I knew was going to happen next. The door separating the cells from the office would burst open and angry, drunken men would stream into the corridor. They'd unlock my cell and drag me out, probably beating me all the way to the street whenever one of them could get in a lick. Then they'd take me to wherever the hanging was to be, and put a rope around my neck and raise me up. It wouldn't be quick. I'd probably die by strangulation, slowly, painfully.

I felt like throwing up. The men in the other cells were utterly silent now. No one said a word. I couldn't even hear them breathe.

I prayed. That the marshal, the sheriff, and their deputies would be able to hold the jail. That they'd try to hold the jail and not simply make a pretense of it. I remembered the marshal's face and his steady eyes. I tried to convince myself that he would really try.

There was a lot of shouting now in the office on the other side of the wooden door that separated it from the cells. Another shotgun blast boomed out.

Then, suddenly, there was a silence as shocking as the uproar had been before. It went on and on. A man in one of the other cells breathed, "I'll bet that blast went right into them. That's why they quieted down so quick."

The marshal's voice, in the complete silence, was clearly audible. "Break it up! Get out of here or the same thing is going to happen to some more of you!"

The noise began again, growing slowly from the complete silence. But there were no more shotgun blasts, and I knew the mob had retreated into the street.

They had been turned back and some of them had been either hurt or killed. They would probably not try to storm the jail again.

I tried to decide what Rafe was likely to do now. It didn't take me long to decide. Failing to get the mob to do his dirty work, he'd simply do it himself. Preferably in a way that would let the blame fall on some member of the mob.

I glanced at the window, knowing that there was absolutely no doubt now that within a few minutes the glass would break. A rifle muzzle would poke its way in and flame and smoke would burst from it.

I glanced at the lantern hanging in the corridor. It was

beyond the reach of anyone. I considered yelling for the marshal, but decided he probably wouldn't hear me over the roar of noise in the street.

I was on my own. Swiftly I dragged my cot over near the cell door. There were blankets on it and a pillow. I grabbed the slop pail and partially flattened it. I put it under the blankets, along with the pillow, trying to arrange them so that they would look like someone was under them. I took off my nearly worn-out boots and placed them at the foot of the cot, arranging the blanket over their tops. It didn't look very real, but the light was bad and Rafe would be in a hurry. I had to count on that.

I didn't know how he'd know which cell I was in, but I knew he would. He'd have wormed it out of one of the deputies, or out of the marshal or the sheriff. However he had managed it he'd know.

The man in the next cell asked, "What do you think you're doing?"

"Trying to make that look like me. That window's going to break in a few minutes and a rifle muzzle's going to be poked in here. I figure he'll think I'm on that cot and shoot at it instead of me." I crossed the cell and positioned myself directly below the barred window.

The man said, "You really didn't shoot Spence, did you?"

"No, sir. I told you that."

"Who's this guy that's after you?"

"Rafe Joslin. The foreman on my father's ranch."

The man in the next cell retreated to a place against the damp stone wall of his cell. The others, who had heard our conversation, tried to get into locations that would be out of the line of fire.

Now there was nothing to do but wait. My breathing was short and shallow. My hands were shaking and so were my knees. I knew this would be only another temporary reprieve. But maybe, just maybe, the marshal or one of the deputies would be able to get out and around the building before Rafe could get away.

I could hear, in the utter silence, voices inside the marshal's office. I couldn't hear what was said. Once I heard a man cry out with pain, and another time I heard a groan. I supposed the wounded were being carried away.

I wondered how many men had been hurt by that shotgun blast and if any had been killed. There was still some noise in the street in front of the jail but not nearly as much as before. The members of the mob had been sobered to see some of their number hurt. They knew, now, that the marshal meant what he had said. He didn't intend to give up the jail. He didn't intend to give up any of his prisoners.

I felt fairly sure now that I wasn't going to be lynched. But I still wasn't out of trouble. I still was charged with the murder of Spence Frazier, and there was still a good chance I'd be convicted if I went to trial.

The man in the next cell said softly, "Kid, I think you're wrong."

"No. I know him and I know he'll come." I was listening intently and I thought I heard something scuff against the outside rock wall of the jail. I held my breath.

There was a long silence and then I heard the scuff again, only this time it sounded like a boot grating on the rocky ground. I whispered, "He's there."

Inside the cells it was so quiet I could hear the breathing of the man in the cell next to mine. I realized I was still holding my breath. I let it sigh slowly out, then drew another one.

The sound of the shattering window was so loud in the silence that I started violently. The first shattering sound was followed by a second and a third as the rifle muzzle poked out all the window panes.

Shards of glass showered down on me. I ducked my head and, when I looked up again, I saw the muzzle of the rifle less than two feet above my head.

It fired, the sound in this small, enclosed space deafening. Acrid black powdersmoke billowed across my cell, reaching as far as the cot, which had twitched as the bullet struck.

I was looking up and, suddenly, I knew there was something I could do. Rafe's left hand was visible on the forestock of the gun. He fired a second time just as I leaped up and grabbed for his wrist.

I felt both hands close on it. He tried to pull back, but I was hanging onto it now, letting my weight pull it through the window and down. I felt my hands begin to slip and I let out a howl that could probably be heard for blocks. "Marshal! Marshal! In back of the jail, quick!"

The man in the next cell said, "Hold on, kid, you got him now!"

My hands were slipping farther down on Rafe's wrist. In a moment they were going to slip clear off. Rafe was pulling back as hard as he could.

I put every last ounce of my remaining strength into holding on. I told myself, "Just another second. Just another second and you can let go."

Rafe was cursing me in a voice so filled with hatred that it turned me cold. The man in the next cell bawled, "Marshal! Around in back! Quick, for God's sake! Quick!"

Rafe let go of the rifle and it clattered to the floor of my cell. And then I heard the sounds of footsteps grating on the ground outside the window of my cell. And I heard the marshal's voice, "All right, you. Move and you're dead!"

I still would not let go, even though Rafe had stopped

trying to pull away, until the marshal called into the window, "You can let go now, kid. We've got him."

I let go and slid to the floor of my cell. I was bathed with sweat and shaking all over. My hands and arms ached. It seemed forever, but it couldn't have been more than a few minutes before the door opened and the marshal came in, herding Rafe ahead of him, a shotgun muzzle in Rafe's back. A deputy came around the two and unlocked my cell door. "Come on out, kid. We'll put him in instead."

I picked up my boots and Rafe's rifle and went out into the corridor. The marshal shoved Rafe inside. He slammed and locked the door. As I went by his cell door, Rafe turned and looked straight at me, his eyes murderous.

I walked along the corridor toward the office. The marshal said, "Not much doubt about it now. He killed Spence and tried to put the blame on you."

"Then I can go?"

"Wait a few minutes until I go tell that damned mob you didn't do it and that we've got the right man in jail." He went through the smashed door and into the street.

Learning that they had been wrong and had almost lynched the wrong person calmed the mob as nothing else could have done. They didn't even seem interested in turning their wrath on Rafe. They began to melt away.

The marshal said, "You can go now, son."

I sat down and pulled on my boots. I asked, "Any chance that he'll get off?"

"Not a chance. He'll hang within a week."

I picked up the rifle and went out into the street. There was a cold breeze blowing down off the high, snowy peaks. I doubted if I'd ever see Standing Bear again.

There were two figures waiting in a doorway half a block from the jail. One of them came running toward me, and I caught her in my arms.

It was over. Susan was crying hysterically and holding me as if she never intended to let me go again.

I'd never wanted to kill Rafe and I was suddenly glad I hadn't had to. I said, "Think you could talk your ma into coming to Wyoming?"

"I think I could."

"Let's get started, then." We walked along the street to Mrs. Overman. Then the three of us walked up the street toward the bakery that had never gotten started and now never would, unless Mrs. Overman was able to sell the idea of starting a bakery to someone else in town. We'd stay here for Spence's funeral. And until Rafe had been executed. Then we'd be going home. *10-4*